THE PERILOUS PROTECTOR

Miss Gillian Ashley encountered Lord Oliver Bain on her very first night in London—when he rushed to her defense as she fought off an assailant in the disreputable district into which she had foolishly strayed.

Gillian looked upon Lord Bain as her savior then—before she learned the truth about him.

Lord Oliver Bain was the most eminent rake in all of society. And what Gillian had to fear was that far from coming to her rescue, he could so easily be planning her ruin, establishing her as the type of young lady whom all too many gentlemen would love to love—and none dare marry. . . .

Scandal's Daughter

SIGNET Regency Romances You'll Enjoy

MARGARET SUMMERVILLE

SCANDAL'S DAUGHTER

A SIGNET BOOK

NEW AMERICAN LIBRARY

one

"Damn your eyes, Bain," growled the stout red-faced gentleman, glaring across the card table like a belligerent bull. "You can't leave now!"

The fifth Earl of Bain smiled, his clear brown eyes alight with amusement. "What's wrong, Baxter, do you want me to win all of your money from you?"

Baxter muttered an obscenity and the other gentlemen at the table laughed.

One of the gentlemen, a curly-haired, effeminate dandy, shook his head. "I for one am quite glad to see you go, Bain. You are having the devil's own luck tonight."

Lord Bain smiled again, stood up, and pocketed his winnings. "Well, then, gentlemen, if you will excuse me, I must be going." The gentlemen at the table did not object to Bain's leaving. After shouting for more wine, they returned to their cards.

It was indeed an early hour for his lordship to be leaving. Most gentlemen stayed at the gaming tables until dawn, or at least until their credit ran out. However, Bain, who was having a most profitable evening, was becoming increasingly bored with the game. He did not enjoy winning so easily and especially to fools like Horace Baxter.

As the earl made his way past several noisy tables, a woman suddenly appeared before him. The woman's face was painted in a rather outrageous fashion and she wore a low-cut, pink gauze gown. She smiled boldly up at him and touched his arm.

"You're leaving so soon, guv'nor? Perhaps you'd like some company?" She winked and gave his arm a squeeze, but was disappointed when he absently shook his head. He would have continued on but she kept hold of his arm.

"But we could 'ave some fun," she protested. "I promise, guv'nor."

Bain turned and looked at her more closely. Underneath the paint and powder he saw a girl of fifteen or sixteen. His gaze went from the girl to the tawdry opulence of their surroundings, and he was filled with a feeling of self-disgust. His lordship frowned and, fishing in his pocket, pulled out a gold coin. He gave it to the girl and abruptly left.

The earl was glad when he finally escaped outside. After the staleness of the gaming establishment, it was good to breathe in the cool night air. As he stood surveying the dark street, a ragged, dirty-faced boy hurried up to him.

"Are you leaving, m'lord? Should I call your groom?"

The earl nodded and flipped the boy a coin. The boy looked at the coin and, discovering it was a half-crown, grinned. "I'll fetch him straight away, m'lord," he said, scurrying off and thinking his lordship must be queer in the head to dispense of his blunt so freely.

If not exactly queer in his head, his lordship was in a decidedly strange mood that night. He stood on the street, lost in rather melancholy musings. The earl was, in fact, growing heartily sick of his life: the gaming, the women, the very idleness of it. He frowned. Perhaps he should leave London and go to the country for a few weeks. However, the thought of going to Castle Bain merely depressed him more. There were few happy associations for him there anymore.

Lord Bain's bleak thoughts were suddenly interrupted by a commotion on the next block. He peered up the street ahead of him and espied two figures struggling in the darkness. One of the figures cried out in a feminine voice, and Bain hurried to her rescue. However, as he got close to them, he saw it was not the woman who needed rescuing but her attacker. She was a tall woman, several inches taller than her attacker, and she was swinging her fists at him with unabandoned ferocity.

"How dare you, you villain!" she cried, and proceeded to shout a string of most unladylike epithets at him as she threw a resounding punch at his stomach.

Her attacker, a short, skinny man with the face of a ferret, cried out in pain and, holding his hands out protectively in front of him, cowered from the unexpected feminine fury.

"Ow! Don't 'it me, miss," he whimpered. "I'm sorry, miss, ow, truly I am." He suddenly noticed Bain's presence and cried out, " 'Elp me, guv'nor, she'll kill me, she will. Ow! Please, guv'nor!" he pleaded.

Lord Bain was enjoying the scene tremendously, but reluctantly decided that he had better restrain the woman or she might indeed kill the ferret-faced fellow. Bain reached out and put a hand on her shoulder. "I think you can stop—" he began, but was cut off abruptly when she turned toward him and unleashed her fury on him. He managed to grab and hold her wrists, but she struggled in his grasp like a wild creature caught in a trap. Bain was amazed by her strength as she continued to struggle with him.

While his lordship was trying to restrain the young lady, her attacker did not stay to thank Providence or his rescuer, but ran off into the night.

"Be still, madam," Bain was saying to the struggling creature in his arms. "I'm trying to help you."

She responded by kicking him in the shin.

Bain cursed. "Damn you, you hellcat," he shouted, shaking her, "listen to me."

She stopped struggling and looked defiantly at him. It was the first good look he had of her face, and Bain was somewhat disconcerted to find the wild "hellcat" was merely a girl, and a very attractive one at that.

A connoisseur of female beauty, the earl could not fail to note that the young woman held so firmly in his grasp was as lovely as any of the ladies who graced the highest circles of society. Although her features were a trifle off the mark of classical perfection, her dazzling blue eyes and long dark curls combined to form a most harmonious picture.

"You will find I have little money," she said, and he was surprised to find that she spoke in a cultivated voice that had a hint of a Scottish accent.

"Good God, chit. I do not intend to rob you. Indeed, I have come to your rescue."

"My rescue? Then you are not in league with that . . . that person?"

He released her arms. "I assure you I am not."

"But you have allowed that felon to escape to prey upon other helpless females."

A slight smile appeared on Bain's face. "Other helpless females? Had I not come along, you would doubtlessly have pummeled the man to death. By God, I've never seen a girl with such a wicked punch. If you were a man, you would be a champion in the ring."

"I should be no such thing. I do not approve of fisticuffs. Such sport is barbaric."

Bain shook his head. "An odd attitude for a female pugilist."

She regarded him indignantly. "I was only trying to protect myself. I did not expect to be attacked by some ruffian my first day in London."

"Day, miss? By my reckoning it is nearly one o'clock. What in God's name is a girl like you doing out on the street at this time of night?"

She looked suddenly distressed. "One o'clock? Oh, I have made a muddle of it. I have been wandering about for hours and am hopelessly lost. Perhaps you could tell me how to get to High Beckley Square."

"High Beckley Square? I am afraid, miss, that it is some five miles distant."

"Oh, dear. That is a very long way."

Although Bain was scarcely given to humanitarian impulses, he was not so hardhearted that he could remain unmoved by the young woman's plight. From her speech and the cut of her well-worn traveling dress, he had judged her to be a lady of quality. The fact that she was seeking High Beckley Square, one of London's more fashionable sections, seemed to confirm this. What she was doing here at such an hour was a mystery to him.

"If you will permit me, I have a carriage waiting and would be happy to escort you."

The relief on her face was enormous. "Would you, sir? I should be most grateful." She hesitated. "But I do not know who you are."

"I am Oliver Bain, Earl of Bain."

"Oh, how do you do." She extended her hand, and Bain took it gallantly although he was conscious that polite introductions under such circumstances were quite ludicrous.

"My name is Gillian Ashley, Lord Bain."

"Well, Miss Ashley, it is getting very late, and now that we are properly acquainted, I shall deliver you to your destination. I am quite familiar with High Beckley Square. Might I ask whom you are seeking?"

Gillian Ashley nodded. "Sir Hewitt Gambol."

It took all of Lord Bain's considerable self-control to keep his astonishment from registering on his face. Sir Hewitt Gambol was an aging roué who had been the most notorious rake of his time. Even in an age when the vices of gentlemen were well tolerated, Sir Hewitt's excesses had so alienated the rest of his class that his name was scarcely mentioned in polite circles. Bain was frankly puzzled. What could this seemingly innocent young woman want with Sir Hewitt Gambol?

"Why are you looking at me like that, my lord?"

The earl frowned. "It is only that respectable young ladies do not associate with Sir Hewitt Gambol."

She smiled at him for the first time. "But you see, sir, I am not at all respectable." She paused and regarded him closely. "And Sir Hewitt Gambol is my natural father."

Oliver Bain had thought that he had seen so much in his thirty-two years that he had lost the ability to be surprised, but Miss Gillian Ashley's announcement that her father was Sir Hewitt Gambol genuinely amazed him. Young ladies simply did not admit such things. Indeed, most young ladies of his acquaintance would have had an attack of vapors at the slightest hint of such matters. Miss Ashley, it seemed, was a most uncommon girl.

He was somewhat acquainted with Sir Hewitt, having once spent several hours at the gaming tables with him. Bain did not dislike the man, which was unusual, since he disliked most of his acquaintances, but he found it difficult to believe that Gambol could have fathered the very attractive Miss Ashley, who was now seated beside him in his carriage.

Bain thought of Gambol's florid puffy face, bulbous red nose, and bulging belly that reflected a lifetime of dissipation. Now, crippled by gout, Gambol no longer frequented the gaming houses and prize fights where Bain had so often seen him. The earl remembered that some years ago he had been walking with his mother when Sir Hewitt passed by in his carriage. The countess had viewed Gambol's bloated face with scorn and had nodded knowingly. "The wages of sin, Oliver," she had said, hoping her son would heed the obvious lesson.

Bain frowned as he always did at the thought of his mother. He knew too well how she disapproved of him and how he constantly disappointed her. It had always been so, and now that he had succeeded to his brother's title, she was even more disappointed with him. Bain knew very well that she resented his taking his brother's place. After all, she blamed him for Edgar's death. His lordship's expression grew very grim.

Gillian Ashley noted Bain's sudden melancholy, but she was too exhausted to think much about it. She leaned back against the leather carriage seat and was grateful to sit down after so much walking. She looked out the carriage window at the darkened London streets dimly lit by street lamps and closed her eyes. The *clip-clop* of the horses' hooves on the cobblestones was a very reassuring sound, and the steady cadence of the hoofbeats nearly lulled her to sleep.

Fighting to stay awake, she shook her head, yawned, and looked over at Lord Bain, who was lost in thought and seemingly oblivious to her presence. She studied Bain carefully, noting his elegant evening clothes and the snowy cravat tied ornately beneath his chin. Gillian thought he was a very handsome man even if he did have a rather arrogant look about him and was something of a dandy. One could tell that by the gold quizzing glass that hung from a satin ribbon around his neck and also by the elaborate arrangement of his curling brown hair.

Gillian shifted in her seat and Bain looked over at her. "I'm afraid I have been poor company."

"Indeed not, sir. I am grateful for some time to think. Are we nearing High Beckley Square?"

Bain nodded. "It is not far." He paused. "Have you seen Sir Hewitt recently?"

"I have never seen him, my lord."

"Never?"

"Not even once. Indeed, I have only learned of his

identity a few days ago. I do not believe he knows of my existence."

"Good Lord. You don't mean you intend to call upon a man you have never met, a man who knows nothing of your existence, in the middle of the night and announce that you are his daughter?"

Gillian nodded. "I know it is not a good hour for paying calls."

Bain laughed. "It is certainly not."

Gillian looked thoughtful. "I have little choice, Lord Bain. I know of nowhere else I can go."

It later amazed Bain that he did not simply shrug and hurriedly desert the young lady at Gambol's doorstep. He was not one to involve himself in other people's problems. Yet he shouted to his driver to pull over and looked at the young woman beside him. "It will not do at all, Miss Ashley. You shall stay tonight at my cousin Meg's house. It is very close."

"Oh, I couldn't! I could not impose on your cousin. Not at such an hour."

"My dear girl, I doubt that Meg has yet retired, and she will be overjoyed to help you."

"No, I could not ask a complete stranger to help me."

"And isn't Sir Hewitt a complete stranger?"

Gillian shrugged. "I suppose he is."

"And I assure you you will receive a much better reception from Meg Fairfax than ever you would get from Sir Hewitt Gambol. Let's have no more about it. Harry! Go to Lady Fairfax's house." The carriage started off again and Gillian felt too tired to argue. Her eyes began to close, and minutes later Bain felt a gentle pressure on his shoulder and looked over to find Gillian Ashley's head upon his shoulder and the young lady fast asleep.

Lady Meg Fairfax sat at her dressing table patiently suffering the ungentle brushing of her long blond hair by her maid. It had been a rather trying day for Lady Fairfax, for she had spent most of the day visiting her husband's relatives. Lord Fairfax had a woeful shortage of tolerable relations, and she sighed.

"Is something wrong, m'lady?"

"I am tired, is all. I think that is enough brushing."

"But I'm not done—"

"I said it is enough," said Lady Fairfax with unaccustomed severity, and her maid nodded obediently.

"Good night, m'lady."

Lady Fairfax was relieved to be alone at last, but just as she was about to get into bed, the maid returned.

"Pardon, your ladyship, but Mr. Hull says there's visitors."

"Visitors?"

"Master Oliver, or I should say Lord Bain, and a lady."

"My cousin here at this hour? Oh, very well, I shall see him. Fetch me my dressing gown." Fearing some calamity, Lady Fairfax hurried down the stairs to the drawing room.

"Meg! I am sorry to call at such an hour."

"Oliver, what is wrong?"

"Nothing whatsoever. It is only that I thought Miss Ashley might stay here tonight."

"Miss Ashley?" Lady Fairfax looked questioningly at Gillian.

"Yes, Meg, this is Miss Ashley. Miss Ashley, Lady Fairfax."

"How do you do," said Gillian, feeling quite embarrassed. "I am so sorry to trouble you. I did not wish to come, but Lord Bain insisted."

"That I did, Meg. You always were one to help those in need, and the girl is exhausted."

Lady Fairfax nodded. "You do look tired, my dear. I'll have my maid show you to a room. We shall talk in the morning."

"You are very kind, ma'am." Gillian smiled and then followed a servant from the room.

When she had gone, Meg Fairfax regarded her cousin

strangely. "What is this, Oliver? Who is that girl? Not one of your paramours I trust?"

"Certainly not. She's but a child."

"Then who is she?"

"I'm not sure. I found her wandering about looking for Sir Hewitt Gambol."

"Good God. Not one of his bits of muslin?"

"Indeed not. She claims to be his daughter." Bain expected that this news would provoke a reaction from his cousin, and he was not disappointed.

"You don't mean that . . . Good heavens. Of course! She must be Caroline Guildford's daughter. She married Rowland Ashley. You must remember the scandal."

"Which scandal is this, Meg?"

"The divorce! You must remember. We spoke of nothing else for weeks and weeks."

Lady Fairfax looked puzzled and then began counting on her fingers. "That would have been in 1792—no, '93. Good heavens, was it so long ago? Twenty years. I can hardly believe it. Even so, I don't see how you could have forgotten."

"My dear Meg, may I remind you I was but twelve years old at the time and away at Eton?"

"Oh, dear, Oliver, it is very bad of you to remind me how much older I am than you. But come and sit down. I shall tell you about it."

Lord Bain joined his cousin on the sofa. "Now what was this scandal all about?"

Meg Fairfax loved nothing better than gossip and she found herself relishing the opportunity to enlighten her cousin. "I was slightly acquainted with Caroline Guildford. Her father was Lord Guildford, a Scottish baron. She was the prettiest girl. Her daughter's pretty, too, of course, but Caroline Guildford was the loveliest creature. Oh, we were all jealous of her. She had so many suitors and she was so gay and witty. And how she could ride!

"One day, when I was at court there was a hunting party. Oh, dear. I am digressing, aren't I? I shall come to the point. Caroline was only seventeen and had twenty offers of marriage. Twenty! Can you imagine? And whom should she choose but Rowland, Viscount Ashley. I must say it was surprising. She could have married anyone, but she married him.

"Now, I was never well acquainted with him, but everyone knows he is a stodgy, ungenerous fellow. He and Caroline were totally unsuited."

"But what of Sir Hewitt?"

"I am getting to that, Oliver. Sir Hewitt was quite dashing in those days. You would never believe it now, but then he was so handsome and had a kind of roguish charm that many ladies had a *tendre* for him. I was one who did not, I must add.

"The Ashleys were staying at the country home of one of Lord Ashley's cousins—I forget who it was, but it doesn't matter—and Sir Hewitt was there too. It seems one thing led to another. Caroline was very young and high-spirited and very unhappy in her marriage. She was also, quite unfortunately, indiscreet. Her husband came upon her writing to Sir Hewitt. They say he made a terrible scene. He searched her room and found a number of letters to her from Sir Hewitt. Poor Caroline.

"As you might imagine, Ashley was furious. He quickly divorced her. It was a very messy business, Oliver. It seems he was able to obtain plenty of evidence of her infidelity. After the divorce her father took Caroline off to Scotland and she was never seen in London again. There was a rumor that she had had a child, but I had never thought it true."

"But what of Sir Hewitt?"

"Surely you've heard of the duel?"

"No, what happened?"

"Ashley called Sir Hewitt out. It was silly of him, for he

was not a very good shot while Sir Hewitt was something of a marksman. Sir Hewitt shot him and it was a miracle he survived. After he recovered, Ashley retreated to his country estate, where he has remained ever since. He remarried again two or three years later. You may recall the present Lady Ashley—such an odious woman—and that daughter of hers, Christobel Stourbridge, is such a detestable young lady. But then you are acquainted with Mrs. Stourbridge."

Bain nodded. "I must say, Meg, this has been a most enlightening evening."

"And enlightening for me, Oliver."

"And what is that?"

"It was most interesting to find you acting the part of a gallant knight helping this poor damsel in distress."

"Don't talk rubbish, Meg."

Lady Fairfax laughed.

"I will be going. I have disrupted your sleep long enough. Thank you for taking her in, Meg."

"I am glad to do so, Oliver, for things were getting very dull around here. But you must come to see me tomorrow. We must dissuade the girl from attempting to see Sir Hewitt."

Bain nodded and, rising from the sofa, kissed his cousin's hand. "I'll be here, Meg. Good night." The earl turned and departed, and Lady Fairfax, although she was now not in the least sleepy, went straight to bed.

two

Gillian Ashley opened her blue eyes and glanced around the room. It took her a few moments to realize where she was. Gillian smiled. Yes, it was true. She was actually in London and had spent the night in this elegant town house, the guest of a kind and obviously very well-to-do society lady.

"Good morning, miss." A maid had entered the room and went to pull open the draperies.

"Good morning. Is it very late?"

" 'Tis near ten o'clock, miss."

"Oh, dear, I have nearly slept the day away."

The maid repressed a smile. She was accustomed to ladies and gentlemen sleeping until well into the afternoon. London society kept very late hours.

"I daresay Lady"—Gillian searched her memory for her hostess's name—"Lady Fairfax will think me a slugabed."

"But her ladyship hae just risen herself, miss. She'll nae think that."

The maid's distinct Highland bur made Gillian smile. "You're Scottish! So am I! Partly, anyway. Where are you from?"

"Frae Inverness."

"Then you are a very long way from home. However did you get to London?"

The maid regarded Gillian with a trace of surprise. She did not expect upper-class ladies to take any notice of her. "Well, miss, 'twas poor times at home with too many mouths to feed, so I went down tae Edinburgh tae find work. I found a place with Sir John Ferguson and came down tae London when Sir John come tae work with the prime minister. But soon after that the master was sent to India! Well, miss, London is one thing, India quite another. I was nae ready to live among heathen savages. 'Tis bad enough living among the English. It was time to find a new position, and here I am."

"And what do you think of London by . . . Oh, I don't even know your name."

"Mary MacDonald, miss. I think it is a fine-enough city for the English."

Gillian laughed. "Well, perhaps one day you will return to Scotland. I hope I shall, but London is very exciting."

Mary MacDonald was about to comment but caught herself. One had to guard oneself against too much familiarity with one's betters. "Shall I help ye dress?"

"Yes, thank you very much, Mary." Gillian tried to sound as though she were accustomed to ladies' maids, for she had never had a personal maid herself. She had been very small when her grandfather the Baron Guildford had died. His successor was her mother's cousin, who made it very clear they were no longer welcome at the ancestral home. And so Lady Caroline Ashley had taken her daughter and moved to Edinburgh, where she lived simply on a small inheritance. Their household in Edinburgh had been quite tiny, and when her mother's inheritance had been used up, they had been virtually penniless. It was then Gillian who did the cooking and cleaning in the shabby rooms they had leased. They had not been able to afford servants for some time before her mother's death.

After dressing in her best and nearly threadbare morning dress and allowing Mary to dress her dark hair, Gillian

SCANDAL'S DAUGHTER / 19

thanked the Scottish maid enthusiastically and proceeded down the stairway to the dining room. There she found Lady Fairfax scrutinizing the newspaper and delicately munching upon a buttered scone.

"Good morning, my dear. I trust you slept well." Meg Fairfax put down the paper and looked encouragingly at Gillian.

"Thank you, Lady Fairfax, I slept very well indeed. In truth, I cannot recall a more comfortable bed. You have been too kind, ma'am."

"Nonsense. Now do get yourself some breakfast." Meg nodded toward the sideboard, where a grand display of platters and silver chafing dishes held an array of food that made Gillian nearly gasp with delight. She took up a plate and began to load it with eggs and sausages and a good-sized kipper, and when she sat down at the table, she looked sheepishly from her pltae to Meg Fairfax.

"Perhaps I have taken rather a lot."

"I am only too glad to see a girl with a hearty appetite."

Gilllian needed no further encouragement and started on the food. "It is excellent."

"Thank you. I do acknowledge that cook is unsurpassed in the realm of breakfast."

Gillian nodded and continued to eat, and Meg Fairfax took a sip of tea. The younger woman's obvious delight with the food amused her. It seemed young Miss Ashley was not used to dining so well. Meg took the opportunity to study her guest more carefully. Yes, she was a very pretty girl, though a trifle thin and rather pale. A few good meals would change that. Her dress was awful, thought Meg, and yet there was something about her that made one forget about her unfashionable attire.

Gillian glanced over at Meg and smiled. Lady Fairfax smiled in return and noted that Miss Ashley had the most attractive smile. It transformed her prettiness into a dazzling beauty, and Lady Fairfax did not doubt that few gentlemen could remain unmoved when faced with that vibrant smile.

"I must say again how grateful I am that you have taken me in."

"My dear girl, do cease thanking me. I know I am a person of Christian virtue."

"But you are good to take me, a perfect stranger, into your home in the middle of the night. And your cousin is the kindest gentleman."

"Oliver Bain the kindest gentleman? I daresay few would agree with you on that. But he is my cousin, and in spite of what you may hear, he is a good sort of man. It is most fortunate that Oliver came upon you when he did. It was not a very wise thing for you to be wandering about town by yourself like that at such an hour."

"I know that very well. It was extremely muddleheaded of me, but I thought I would be able to walk to my father's house."

"You mean Sir Hewitt Gambol?"

Gillian nodded. "Is his house very far from here? I do not wish to trouble you any further, and if I had directions, I could walk there."

"My dear child, I am not acquainted with the location of Sir Hewitt Gambol's house, and I am of the opinion that you should not become acquainted with it either."

"But he is my father."

"Then why did he not send someone for you? He is not a poor man."

"He does not know I am coming." Gillian hesitated. "You see, Lady Fairfax, he does not even know I am his daughter."

Meg's eyes opened wide. "And you intended to go to him, announce the fact, and be welcomed with open arms?"

"I don't know how he will react, but he is my father and he does have some duty toward me."

"But why have you not attempted to contact him before?"

"Why, I only learned who he was last week."

"Last week?"

Gillian nodded. "You see, my mother never told me why she left Lord Ashley. Oh, I had bits and pieces of the story. I knew he and my mother had quarreled violently and she had been sent away. I heard this from one of my grandfather's servants. My mother later explained that they had been divorced. I must say I found it very hard to understand, as she would give me no details, but it was so painful for her to speak of it. She died a year ago."

"My poor dear. What did you do?"

"We had had very little money left, but I stayed on in Edinburgh taking in students to tutor in French."

"You stayed by yourself?"

Gillian nodded. "I held out as long as possible, but finding tutoring did not bring in enough money, I decided to go to my cousin Lord Guildford for help." Gillian smiled ruefully. "I should not have bothered. After all, it was he who had sent us away as soon as he succeeded my grandfather as Lord Guildford."

"He sounds like a horrible man."

Gillian nodded and brought a forkful of food to her mouth. "He is an uncharitable wretch. When I arrived asking for help, he grudgingly allowed me to stay the night. In the morning he suggested I ask assistance from my true father, Sir Hewitt Gambol. As I had never heard of Sir Hewitt, this was quite a revelation to me."

"This cousin of yours sounds perfectly dreadful."

"Perhaps I should be grateful to him for telling me the truth."

"But your mother never spoke of Sir Hewitt?"

"Never, my lady. But after learning of the truth, I returned to Edinburgh, and in going through my mother's papers, I came across a letter from Sir Hewitt. I knew then it was true. Sir Hewitt Gambol is my father.

"Surely I can get no poorer reception from Sir Hewitt than from Lord Guildford. I made inquiries in Edinburgh about him and learned that he had never married. I need not worry about shocking his wife or children."

"That is a blessing, but, my dear, Sir Hewitt is not known for his generosity. I do not know how he would receive you."

"In any case, I must find out for myself. I must see him."

Meg Fairfax shook her head. "Is there no one else you might ask for help? I assure you seeing Sir Hewitt would be a mistake. I must be frank with you. Sir Hewitt is not accepted in polite society."

"But neither am I, so that does not signify. You act as if my father is some sort of monster. I refuse to believe it. My mother was a fine woman, and if she loved Sir Hewitt, there must have been much good in him."

"My dear girl, I do not know about that. I do know that Sir Hewitt Gambol is not a fit sort of man with whom a young girl might associate. He is addicted to drink and gaming and . . . women of easy virtue. There are things said of him that I could not repeat to you. I do not say these things from spite or malice, but because I think you would be better off avoiding this man. Acknowledging him as your father would do you no good in society, I assure you."

"I do not care for society's opinion, ma'am. It would be most unfortunate if I did. No, I do not expect Sir Hewitt to be overjoyed to see me, but at least he could assist me a little. I need only enough money to survive until I can find a position as a governess. Then I shall be able to earn my living and will need no one's help."

"You wish to become a governess?"

"I see little else I can do. I was a very good student and my French is very good."

Meg Fairfax frowned. She could think of few less gloomy pictures than life as a governess. Although she had known Gillian Ashley for scarcely an hour, she could see that the young woman had neither the training nor the temperament for such a life.

"If you are searching for such a position, I believe I would be much better able to help you than Sir Hewitt."

"Would you help me, my lady? I should be very grateful."

"I will help you in any way I can, but I think I can do far better than find you a position as a governess."

"What do you mean, Lady Fairfax?"

"I mean, my dear, that I shall find you a husband."

This pronouncement caused Gillian to regard her benefactor with a startled expression.

"I do believe it is the only solution. You would be miserable as a governess. It is obvious to me that you would be better off married to a good and generous man. I have been so very fortunate myself where husbands are concerned. Lord Fairfax is a wonderful man and I am very fond of him. Yes, indeed, my experience has made me quite favorably disposed to husbands."

"But, Lady Fairfax, I have no fortune and my name is tinged with scandal. No gentleman would be interested in me."

"Do not forget you are a very pleasant and likable young lady, and a very attractive one. I do not doubt that if you were to come out into society, you would have all manner of suitors."

"But, ma'am, you cannot think the result of an adulterous union could be admitted to society."

"Balderdash, my girl. If all those who are the results of adulterous unions were driven from society, there would scarce be enough left to fill any decent-sized ballroom. Don't look so shocked. Adultery is very common in society, although I will admit divorce is not.

"With my patronage I do not think you will have any trouble being accepted. I do not mean to sound immodest, but I have much influence in the highest circles. I do not think we shall have any trouble at all establishing you in society."

"But I do not know if I want to be established. You are kind, Lady Fairfax, but I am not altogether sure I wish to go into society, and I am quite certain that I would not want a husband at the present time."

"Not want a husband? Don't talk nonsense. Every young girl wants a husband." The way Meg Fairfax spoke these words allowed little opportunity for argument. "Do say you will stay with me for a time. It will be such fun."

Although Gillian did not think Meg Fairfax seemed to be thinking very clearly, it was hard to refuse such hospitality. "I should very much like to stay with you a few days, but I could not impose on you any longer. You must not put yourself to any trouble for my sake."

"Trouble? It will be no trouble, my dear. Indeed, we shall be great friends. Now, do finish your breakfast. It is growing cold."

Gillian smiled and resumed eating.

three

O liver Bain entered his mother's London house with the usual feeling of uneasiness. The butler bowed to him respectfully and led him into his mother's sitting room. As always, his mother was sitting in her chair, concentrating on her embroidery. His lordship leaned down and planted a dutiful kiss on his mother's cheek. "Hello, Mama."

"Oliver. I had hoped you would have called on me yesterday."

Lord Bain sat down on the sofa opposite his mother and prepared himself for her usual reproaches.

"I thought you said you would call Tuesday, which, as you know very well, was yesterday."

"I am sorry, Mama, but I don't recall setting a particular day." He glanced around his mother's sitting room and began to feel uncomfortable. It was a dreary little room, and his mother refused to decorate it although the furniture and draperies were worn and old-fashioned. Everywhere about the room were mementos of his elder brother Edgar. Edgar's portrait stared down at him from a prominent place on the wall and a lithograph of Edgar's favorite horse hung beside it. Edgar's prayer book, his silver spurs, and his riding crop sat upon the mantel like offerings upon an altar.

"Are you feeling well, Mama? Perhaps you would like to walk with me in the park this afternoon."

"No, I do not think so, Oliver. I am not feeling well enough, but it is kind of you to ask me."

Lady Bain returned to her embroidery and they sat in silence for a time. The earl glanced up at his brother's portrait and then over at his mother. The dowager countess looked very tired and frail, although she was not yet sixty. She was dressed in mourning as she had continued to do since Edgar's death nearly three years ago. The black dress and cap made her face look very pale.

"I expect you will be spending all day with me Sunday next, Oliver?"

"Sunday next, Mama? I'm not certain what you mean."

Lady Bain looked coldly at her son. "It is the twenty-third of May."

The earl winced as if he had received a blow. The twenty-third of May was the anniversary of Edgar's death.

"Perhaps you have forgotten the significance of that date."

"Of course I had not forgotten. In God's name, how could I forget?"

Lady Bain made a careful stitch in her embroidery. "No, of course you would not forget. He was your brother and he loved you very much, Oliver."

His lordship stood up suddenly. Greatly agitated, he paced across the room and then turned to face his mother. "How long will this go on?"

"What do you mean, Oliver?"

"I mean, how long will you continue to blame me for Edgar's death?"

"You're talking nonsense. I do not blame you. Yes, it was your curricle and your horses, but Edgar himself was driving them. I have never blamed you."

"Dear God, Mama, you have blamed me in every look you have given me for three years now. I did not want him to take the curricle. They were not horses that could be controlled by just anyone."

"But you did allow it, didn't you?"

"He was my elder brother and the Earl of Bain. I could not refuse him!"

Lady Bain placed another stitch in her embroidery and seemed to be fighting back tears.

"Can't you understand that I have felt as much pain as you by his death. He was my brother!" The earl sat down beside his mother and reached out to take her hand.

She snatched it away and looked at him angrily. "You have never given me a day's peace, Oliver. Edgar knew his duty. He never did one thing in his lifetime to sully his noble name. He was not forever dashing out on fast horses, gaming and drinking and throwing his money away on vulgar mistresses. He was good and kind and the best son a mother could ever have had. I was always so proud of him. He was to marry Lady Constance Russell. He knew how dearly I loved Constance." Tears began to fall from Lady Bain's eyes. "And now she has married another and has a sweet little boy. He might have been my grandson."

Oliver Bain stood up and clenched his fists in frustration. He scarcely trusted himself to speak. "And I have brought disgrace to the family name? Is that what you mean, Mother?"

"You have done no honor to it. I had hoped your new responsibilities would curb your dissolute habits."

"Dissolute, madam?"

She looked accusingly at him. "You have always been a great disappointment to me, Oliver."

The earl said not one more word, but left the room. He stormed out of his mother's house and shouted to his groom to get out of the driver's seat of his awaiting phaeton. He jumped into the vehicle and, taking up the whip, lashed savagely at his horses. The phaeton sped away, leaving

Harry behind to make his way back on foot and reflect that his master had an even worse than usual encounter with his mother.

The Earl of Bain was in no better humor by the time he returned to his London town house. The earl's servants were accustomed to their master's black moods and volatile temper, and they quickly realized it was prudent to steer clear of his lordship in his present state.

His lordship's butler, Parker, merely nodded when the earl burst into the house, curtly commanding him to bring a bottle of brandy to the library. Although it was an early hour for brandy, the butler knew that even so much as a slightly raised eyebrow would provoke the wrath of his grim-faced employer.

Parker quickly returned with a bottle of the earl's best brandy. Entering the library, he found his lordship sprawled out in a chair by the fireplace, his brown eyes staring gloomily into space.

Bain looked up at the butler's entrance. "Put it on the table, Parker."

The butler put the tray on the table and then hesitated. The earl scowled. "Well, what is it, man?"

"Nothing, my lord. I was just wondering if your lordship would be needing anything else."

Bain shook his head, and the butler bowed and gratefully retreated from the room. As he closed the library's large oak doors, Parker shook his head sadly. He had little doubt that his master would not stir from the room until he was quite drunk or in need of another bottle.

The earl did seem intent on getting drunk. As soon as Parker exited the room, he poured himself a generous glass of brandy and swiftly downed half of it. He stared at the remaining brandy in his glass and suddenly the disapproving visage of his mother appeared before him. "You have always been a great disappointment to me, Oliver."

Bain swore and took another swig of brandy. What did it matter, anyway? He could never do anything that would please his mother. It had always been that way. Even as a child, nothing he did was ever good enough.

The earl remembered when he was a boy at Eton and had won a prize for an essay he had written. Thinking it would finally make his mother proud of him, he had dashed off an excited letter to her about it. Her cool reply cut him deeply. "One must not brag about one's accomplishments, Oliver," she had admonished him. "And although you have done well on the essay, you must not forget that your Greek and Latin are in much need of improvement."

Bain poured himself another glass of brandy. Of course, it was quite different with his brother Edgar. Edgar had had no need to brag of his accomplishments because his mother was always doing that for him. She was constantly reading his letters out loud and remarking on what a clever boy he was. Few visitors to Castle Bain could escape hearing about the many accomplishments and virtues of the future earl.

Perhaps it would have been easier if Oliver had disliked his brother, but he had always loved and admired Edgar, who was five years his senior. When Bain was a boy, he had practically idolized him. As a result, he had been consumed with guilt by his jealousy of Edgar's favored position in his mother's affections.

No, Edgar had never disappointed his mother. He was never a cause of embarrassment to her like his wayward brother. Edgar had been the model of propriety as the Earl of Bain. He would have married the very respectable Lady Constance Russell and would have given his mother an exceptional brood of grandchildren.

The earl was about to take another drink when the thought of the respectable Lady Constance made him think of another young lady, one who had called herself "not at all respectable." He remembered his first sight of

Miss Gillian Ashley when she was pummeling her unwary attacker, and a slight smile broke through the gloomy expression on his lordship's face.

Sir Hewitt Gambol's daughter! He could still scarcely believe it. And she had meant to march up to the old roué's doorstep and announce herself as his illegitimate offspring. Bain shook his head. She certainly was an unusual young lady. He wondered how she was faring this morning with his cousin Meg. The earl put down his glass quite suddenly and stood up.

When he opened the library door and called for Parker, the butler was quite surprised but hurried to answer his summons.

"Parker, have Harry bring my phaeton. I'm going out again."

"Yes, my lord," said Parker, quite puzzled but at the same time happy at the apparent change in his master's mood. A short time later, the earl took up the reins to his phaeton and left for his cousin's house.

four

W hen the Earl of Bain was ushered into Lady Fairfax's drawing room, he found his cousin in the midst of scrutinizing the fashions of the lastest issue of *Le Beau Monde.* Usually any interruption was unwelcome when her ladyship was thus engaged, but she looked up from the magazine and smiled at him.

"Oliver! How very surprising to see you at such an early hour. I thought you made it a rule never to rise before two o'clock while in town."

The earl smiled. "My dear coz, you know the only rule I make is never to make any rules."

She laughed. "Oh, I know. You are quite incorrigible. But do sit down, Oliver. I must admit I am in a mood to be charitable to you today, for you have done me a great favor."

"Indeed, ma'am? I can scarcely think what it might be."

"Why, bringing Gillian Ashley here last night, of course."

The earl shook his head. "I doubt many ladies would consider it a favor to deposit a complete stranger on their doorstep in the middle of the night. And especially one who claims to be the illegitimate daughter of Sir Hewitt Gambol."

31

"Really, Oliver, you need not remind me of that unfortunate connection. It could prove something of an obstacle in securing the girl a proper husband. But it is not an insurmountable obstacle. I am sure once she is introduced into society, under my patronage, of course—"

"What the devil are you talking about, Meg?"

"Why, about Gillian, of course! Oh, Oliver, it will be such fun bringing her into society. She is such a charming girl—and so very attractive, don't you think? I must say I've already taken quite a fancy to her. I am certain she could make a brilliant match, and I mean to help her."

The Earl of Bain frowned. "And what does Miss Ashley think of your scheme?"

Lady Fairfax laughed. "Oh, she was somewhat skeptical. Said no one would marry her and she didn't know if she even wanted a husband. Can you imagine? She had some foolish notion about finding a post as a governess. A governess, Oliver! Can you imagine a more wretched existence for the girl? She finally consented to stay a few days and I am certain that she will come to her senses." Lady Fairfax smiled. "And I thought it was going to be a dull Season. I really must thank you, Oliver."

The earl was about to make a reply to this comment when the subject of their conversation entered the room.

The earl found that the morning light did nothing to diminish the young lady's beauty. Indeed, he thought she looked even lovelier than he had remembered her. She smiled when she saw him, and the earl found himself experiencing a rather peculiar sensation.

"Gillian, my dear," said Lady Fairfax, motioning her to come in, "Oliver and I were just talking about you."

"I rather feared you might be." She held out her hand to the earl. "Good day, Lord Bain. I can never thank you enough for your help last night."

"It was nothing, Miss Ashley."

"No, it was quite a lot. You and Lady Fairfax have been

so very kind to me, but I don't wish to be of any more trouble to you—"

"Trouble? Nonsense, my girl!" cried Lady Fairfax. "I was just telling Oliver how thankful I was to him for bringing you here last night. Oh, my dear, it will be such a diverting Season, and great fun finding you a husband!"

Gillian looked somewhat embarrassed and turned to the earl. "I fear, my lord, that Lady Fairfax has struck upon the idea of finding me a husband. I told her it was ridiculous. No gentleman would marry me."

"Stuff and nonsense, Gillian," said Lady Fairfax. "You shall have scores of gentlemen wanting to marry you."

Gillian shook her head and smiled. "Any gentleman who would want to marry me, with my background and lack of fortune, would have to be rather bird-witted." She turned again to Bain. "My lord, perhaps you could make her see that such an idea is absurd."

The Earl of Bain smiled. "My cousin is a very determined lady, Miss Ashley. If she has her mind set on finding you a husband, it would not surprise me to see you married within a fortnight."

"You are quite right, Oliver," Lady Fairfax said. "I am a determined lady. I will not have this poor girl become a governess. Good heavens, I shudder at the thought!"

"Really, Lady Fairfax, I doubt it would be as bad as all that. I am not accustomed to luxury. And perhaps if I am frugal and save my wages, someday I could get myself a small cottage and—"

"Please, Gillian!" Lady Fairfax cried in mock horror. "I will hear no more of such plans. Living like some wretched miser, trying to teach a passel of brats whose only goal in life would be to make you miserable. No, Gillian. That is not the life for you. You need not worry about a thing. I will take care of everything and you can stay here as long as you like."

"You are too kind, Lady Fairfax, but I couldn't

possibly impose on you in such a manner. You see, ma'am, I am a rather determined person myself." She smiled. "In fact, some have called me headstrong. You are very generous, but I couldn't continue to take advantage of your generosity. No, I will do what I intended to do. First, I shall go and see my father and then I will inquire about a position."

"You still can't mean to go see Sir Hewitt Gambol?" asked Lady Fairfax in surprise. When Gillian nodded, her ladyship turned to her cousin in exasperation. "Oliver, I have been unable to convince the girl that a visit to Sir Hewitt would be most unwise. Perhaps you could talk some sense into her."

Gillian looked at the earl and he felt obliged to speak. "Meg is right. It would be ill-advised for an innocent girl like yourself to go and see Sir Hewitt. His . . . excesses are quite well known."

"Really, sir," Gillian said somewhat indignantly. "I am not an infant! I am twenty and quite capable of taking care of myself."

The earl raised his eyebrows. "Indeed, ma'am? I do beg your pardon. I did not realize you were so quickly approaching your dotage."

Gillian laughed. "Oh, I am sorry I snapped at you. You have been so very kind. But I do not like people treating me like a child. And I refuse to believe that my father is as wicked as all that."

Lady Fairfax shrugged. "Well, my dear, do not upset yourself over it. We shall discuss it again later. But let us talk about something more pleasant. I thought we could take a trip into town today. What would you think about that?"

"Oh, yes," said Gillian enthusiastically, momentarily forgetting Sir Hewitt at the exciting prospect of an afternoon in the city. "I should very much like to see London." She smiled over at his lordship. "I daresay I wandered through quite a bit of the city last night on my arrival, but I fear it was not the best time to see it."

"I should say not," said Lady Fairfax. "It's very fortunate that Oliver found you. But never mind about that now. We must plan our afternoon. I thought we could start at Smithson's, that's a linen drapers, don't you know, and the finest one in London. And then, of course, we should go and see Madame Bonacieux. Madame Bonacieux is my dressmaker and quite remarkable. And she will be so delighted at having a beautiful young lady like you to show off her gowns. Oh, and I heard that Bentley's has a new stock of bonnets in. Some of the new bonnets are really quite outrageous. I must show you some of them in *Le Beau Monde*." Lady Fairfax grabbed the magazine from the table and began paging through it. "Dear me, where are those bonnets with the fruit on them?" She looked up from the magazine and was surprised to see a look of disappointment on Gillian Ashley's face. "Why, whatever is the matter, my dear?"

"Oh, nothing, ma'am. It's just when you said we were to go into the city I thought you meant we would see some of the sights. I didn't realize you meant we would be going shopping."

Lady Meg Fairfax looked flabbergasted. "The sights?"

Gillian nodded. "You know . . . Westminster Abbey, the Houses of Parliament, the Tower of London. I especially wanted to see the Tower," she said somewhat wistfully.

"The Tower?" Lady Fairfax repeated incredulously. "But, my dear Gillian, no one goes to 'see the sights' except rustics. It is just not done."

"Oh," said Gillian.

The earl was somewhat amused by Gillian's obvious disappointment. She looked like a child who had just received a present and, instead of it being the expected toy, found it was a pair of stockings.

"Really, I can't imagine why anyone wants to see such things anyway," Meg Fairfax was saying. "We shall have much more fun at the shops, my dear, than in some drafty cathedral or hideous dungeon."

The earl laughed. "Come, now, Meg. Not everyone finds history as dull as you do." He turned to Gillian. "If you wish, Miss Ashley, I would be happy to escort you to see the sights some afternoon. That is, if you don't mind being considered a rustic."

Gillian smiled. "Oh, thank you, my lord. I would like that very much."

Lady Fairfax eyed her cousin curiously. It was quite unlike Oliver to be so noble. She had a sudden suspicion about his motives but quickly dismissed it. Although her cousin had had his share of affairs and mistresses, he was not the type to seduce innocent maidens like Gillian Ashley.

"Well, then," she said, "that is settled. You can go to the Tower another day. But today, my dear, we really must go shopping. If you are to be introduced into society, you must have some new clothes."

"I'm afraid, ma'am, that I can't afford any new clothes. I used up most of my money for the journey here."

Lady Fairfax made a gesture of dismissal. "That doesn't signify, my dear. I have money. Quite a bit of it, in fact, and I insist on buying you some clothes."

"But, Lady Fairfax, I couldn't allow you to—"

"Really, Gillian, this arguing is getting tiresome. I want to buy you some new clothes. Won't you allow me that pleasure?"

Gillian finally relented. It was not that the prospect of new clothes was so unwelcome to her. She was well aware that her present wardrobe was quite shabby and old-fashioned. However, she was proud and did not like to take charity.

"Good," cried Lady Fairfax, and again began rummaging through her fashion magazine.

The earl took that for his cue to leave. "Since you ladies have other matters to consider, I will take my leave."

"Yes, Oliver," said Lady Fairfax with a smile, "you are rather in the way right now."

He smiled in return, said good-bye to the ladies, and departed.

It was an uncommonly large crowd at the linen drapers, and Lady Fairfax was none too pleased that they had to wait half an hour to be waited on. However, her ladyship returned to a better humor when she espied some blue gauze that she decided would be just the thing for Gillian's new evening gown. Gillian was amazed at the quantities of cloth that Lady Fairfax bought. She purchased yards and yards of muslin, and each time that Gillian thought Lady Fairfax had made her last purchase, her ladyship's eye fell on another piece of cloth that she insisted on having.

They finally left the crowded shop and proceeded on to Madame Bonacieux's establishment. Madame Bonacieux was one of the most-sought-after dressmakers in London and her shop was evidence of her success. It was quite elegant, with Louis XIV chairs, velvet draperies, and potted palm plants in large brass pots.

Lady Fairfax was immediately recognized as she came through the door, and a lady quickly rushed up to wait on her. Since her ladyship was one of Madame Bonacieux's most important customers, it did not take long for that lady herself to appear before them.

Gillian studied Madame Bonacieux with great interest. She did not at all look like the dressmakers she had seen in Edinburgh. Madame Bonacieux looked like a great lady herself. She was an attractive woman of middle age, and when she spoke to them, it was with a pronounced French accent.

"Ah, Lady Fairfax," she said in a musical voice, "how nice to see you. You are looking quite lovely, my lady."

Lady Fairfax, who was not adverse to flattery, smiled

gratefully at the dressmaker. "Thank you, madame."

"Have you come for a new gown, then, my lady?" asked Madame Bonacieux, quite pleased at the prospect of another profitable commission from her ladyship.

"No, not for myself, madame. But I have brought a young lady who is in need of your excellent work."

"Ah, this pretty young mademoiselle?" asked Madame Bonacieux, smiling at Gillian.

"Yes. This is Gillian Ashley, madame. She is staying with me and needs several gowns made for her. Do you think you could manage it?"

Madame Bonacieux appeared delighted. "Ah, *oui*, my lady. It will be a pleasure to make gowns for the young lady."

Lady Fairfax nodded. "Good. Let me tell you what I had in mind." And the ladies began conferring on Gillian's new wardrobe.

After spending a couple of hours with Madame Bonacieux, Gillian and Lady Fairfax proceeded to several more shops where they purchased four bonnets, a number of shifts, stockings, and other essentials. By this time Gillian was becoming quite exhausted with shopping, and she was glad when Lady Fairfax suggested they stop at a small shop for tea.

"Well, Gillian," said her ladyship as they sat down at a table near the window so they could observe the passersby, "wasn't that great fun? I must say I am quite pleased with everything we bought. And I am certain Madame Bonacieux will make some magnificent gowns for you."

"Yes, I am sure she will. You are really too good, Lady Fairfax, to take me in like you did and now you buy all these things for me."

Her ladyship smiled. "Oh, please don't start on that again, Gillian. I enjoyed buying those things today. And why don't you call me Meg? We are to be friends and I feel positively ancient having you call me Lady Fairfax constantly."

Gillian smiled. "All right, Meg."

"That's better. I must say I feel a bit tired. It is good to rest for a bit and they have the most delicious biscuits here. I must confess that biscuits are a terrible weakness of mine." Lady Fairfax looked around at the other customers in the shop and her gaze rested on a table where two fashionable ladies sat. "Oh, no," she said. "Letitia Cavendish!"

"Who is she?" asked Gillian, following Lady Fairfax's gaze to the other table.

"She is married to the Marquess of Cavendish. I don't know which of them is worse. Letitia Cavendish is an odious woman. Oh, dear, I hope she doesn't see us."

Unfortunately for Lady Fairfax, just as she spoke these words, Lady Cavendish looked directly at her. She waved to her, appeared to say something to her companion, and then both ladies got up from their table and advanced toward them.

"Oh, no," muttered Lady Fairfax under her breath.

After Lady Fairfax's unkind remarks about Lady Cavendish, Gillian was quite surprised when the two women greeted each other as if they were the best of friends.

"Meg Fairfax!" Lady Cavendish cried. "How delightful to see you."

"Letitia," said Lady Fairfax with no less enthusiasm, "how are you? You are looking as wonderful as ever."

"Why, thank you, Meg," said Lady Cavendish. Her ladyship was a petite, somewhat plump lady, with rather piercing blue eyes. She quickly fixed her keen gaze on Gillian, and Lady Fairfax introduced her.

Lady Cavendish in turn introduced her companion, Mrs. Rhodes, a tall silent lady who looked as if she were suffering from indigestion.

"Ashley," repeated Lady Cavendish quizzically. "Are you related to Christobel Stourbridge? She was a Miss Ashley."

"I do not think so, Lady Cavendish," replied Gillian politely. "I have few relations."

Lady Fairfax quickly cut in. "Gillian just recently arrived in town and I am showing her about." She made an abrupt attempt to change the subject. "I say, Letitia, have you seen the new bonnets at Bentley's? I daresay they will be all the rage, but I think they look rather ridiculous."

Lady Cavendish frowned. "Indeed? I just purchased one of them."

Gillian repressed a smile as Lady Fairfax tried to recover from her blunder. "Oh, have you? Of course, my dear, I didn't mean to say they were ridiculous, exactly. Just, well, unusual."

Lady Cavendish eyed her coolly but turned her attention back to Gillian. "So you have just recently arrived in town, Miss Ashley. Where are you from?"

"I am from Edinburgh, Lady Cavendish."

"Edinburgh?" asked Lady Cavendish. "You are Scottish, then?"

Gillian did not like the uncomplimentary tone of this question, but she nodded. "Partly, anyway."

"Oh, dear," said Lady Fairfax, who was still trying to make a diversion. "I do wonder where our tea is? The service here is usually quite good."

Lady Cavendish looked at Lady Fairfax and wondered why she was so eager to change the subject from Miss Gillian Ashley. Who was the girl, anyway? Gillian Ashley. Ashley. Lady Cavendish suddenly had a flash of insight. The girl said she was from Edinburgh. Didn't the scandalous Caroline Ashley go off to Scotland after her divorce? Heavens, it must be some twenty years ago by now, thought her ladyship. She looked closely at Gillian as the details of that scandal returned to her. Lady Caroline had been having an affair with that old reprobate, Sir Hewitt Gambol. Of course, he wasn't an old reprobate then, remembered Lady Cavendish. He was quite dashing. And Viscount Ashley had found out and divorced his wife. It had been a dreadful scandal. Lady Cavendish remembered how no one talked of anything else for months. And wasn't there some rumor that Lady Caroline had had a baby after returning to Scotland? Lady Cavendish looked from Gillian to Lady Fairfax. That lady was discussing the fine weather with Mrs. Rhodes, who appeared to be a lady of few opinions.

Lady Cavendish smiled at a momentary break in this conversation and turned again to Gillian. "I fear I am not acquainted with any Ashleys from Edinburgh. Indeed, I am only acquainted with a few Ashleys." She looked from Gillian to Meg Fairfax. "I was slightly acquainted with Rowland, Viscount Ashley, but have not seen the poor man in, oh, it must be twenty years now. You remember him, don't you, Meg?" When Lady Fairfax blanched at the mention of Rowland Ashley's name, Lady Cavendish smiled in triumph.

She looked at Gillian and found that young lady eyeing her with a somewhat defiant expression. "Of course, my dear, you would be much too young to remember the terrible scandal about Lord Ashley's wife. You cannot be any more than seventeen, surely."

"I have just turned twenty, ma'am," replied Gillian coolly.

"Twenty! Imagine that. I thought you were a miss just out of the schoolroom. Well, I daresay I shall be seeing you again, Miss Ashley. I do hope so." Lady Cavendish turned to her companion. "I think we had best go, Emma." She turned back to Lady Fairfax and Gillian.

"My husband is having a few of his detestable relations over for dinner tonight and I must see that there is no catastrophe in the kitchen."

Both Lady Fairfax and Gillian were glad to see Lady Cavendish depart.

"Oh, dear, what a dreadful woman," said her ladyship as she watched Lady Cavendish and Mrs. Rhodes leave the shop and enter their carriage. "And she is also one of the worst gossips in the kingdom."

Gillian smiled. "Is she? Then I am glad I was able to provide her with some fresh gossip."

Lady Fairfax sighed. She knew Letitia Cavendish well and had little doubt that she would soon have tongues wagging all over the kingdom about Gillian Ashley. But she supposed the girl's identity could not be kept a secret forever. Perhaps it was better to have the business out in the open from the very start. Her ladyship's musings were cut off by the appearance of a girl with their tea, and she and Gillian were soon enjoying an excellent repast of tea and biscuits.

five

"That's a good man, Dawson. Do see those things are taken upstairs. Mary will tell you where to put them."

"Very good, my lady." The footman somehow managed to balance all the parcels that Meg and Gillian had brought home from their shopping expedition. He skillfully made his way up the stairs, and Gillian suspected from his expression that he was quite used to the quantity of items resulting from her ladyship's day of shopping.

Meg Fairfax sat down in one of the drawing-room chairs, quite exhausted. "Oh, my dear Gillian, that was fun, was it not?"

"It was, but, Meg, I can never repay you for those things."

"I do not wish to be repaid. The pleasure of seeing you in one of Madame Bonacieux's gowns will be payment enough. Yes, indeed, I think it was a most successful excursion. That blue gauze will make the most delightful gown for you."

"Please, Meg, I do not feel right having you do so much for me."

"My dear young lady, this is such fun for me. You cannot grudge me the enjoyment of seeing you become a great success in society. I have been so very bored lately and, to tell you the truth, simply dreading the thought of the new Season. But now I am so eager for all the parties. I am doing this for myself as much as for you.

"Now please, as a favor to me, do not persist in telling me how generous I am. I am not a poor woman, I assure you." Lady Fairfax raised a hand to her forehead. "Oh, I have a dreadful headache. It was seeing that odious Lady Cavendish. How I loathe that woman! And that insufferable Emma Rhodes.

"My dear, I do not wish to leave you sitting alone, but would you mind if I retired to my room for a time? I believe a nap would help rid myself of this headache."

"Then by all means go. I shall be fine. Perhaps I shall have a nap later myself."

Meg Fairfax smiled. "Do make yourself at home. Ring the servants if you require anything at all. And Lord Fairfax's library is just through the hallway. Perhaps you would care to see it?"

"Oh, yes, that would be very nice."

After leading her young friend to the library and seeing her become quickly engrossed in her husband's book collection, Lady Fairfax left Gillian and went to her room.

Gillian Ashley, a great book lover, was thrilled at the size and scope of Lord Fairfax's library. After browsing for some time, she settled on a small volume of poetry and then returned to the drawing-room to read.

However, only a short time passed before Gillian's mind began to wander. How fortunate that she would have met Lady Fairfax. Who would have thought that now poor Miss Ashley from Edinburgh had the opportunity to enter society under the auspices of one of society's most prominent hostesses?

Gillian smiled. It was a marvelous opportunity, but she could not allow Lady Fairfax to do any more for her. Her thoughts shifted to Lord Bain and how she had first met him. He must have thought her quite outrageous. Gillian sighed. Yes, a silly outrageous schoolgirl is what he thought of her.

Gillian's mind wandered from Lord Bain to Edinburgh, and she thought of her mother and the tiny rooms where they had lived. She took her reticule from the chair where she had placed it, and took out a paper from the small purse. It was the letter to her mother from Sir Hewitt Gambol dated just days before her birth.

She wondered what sort of man Sir Hewitt was. She reread the letter and sighed. He could certainly not be as bad as everyone said to have written such a letter. It was obvious that he cared very deeply for her mother. Gillian stared at the letter for a while longer and then carefully folded it and returned it to the reticule.

There were so many unanswered questions about her mother and Sir Hewitt. Questions that only he could answer. Gillian stood up abruptly. She had no choice but to see Sir Hewitt Gambol. He was her father and she simply had to see him.

Despite what Meg Fairfax would say, Gillian resolved to go. She took up her bonnet and tied the ribbons carefully under her chin.

"Hull," she said, calling the butler, "if her ladyship comes down, please tell her that I have gone for a walk. I shall be back very soon."

"Would you wish one of the girls to accompany you, miss?"

"Oh, no, Hull, that will not be necessary. I do not intend to go far." Feeling rather dishonest, but knowing she had to find Sir Hewitt, Gillian left the house and made her way down the street. After receiving directions on how to find High Beckley Square from a most helpful young constable, she walked briskly toward her destination.

Long walks around Edinburgh had been Gillian's favorite pastime, and the two-mile distance to High Beckley Square did not seem at all far to her. The weather was good and the streets filled with interesting sights, and it did not seem so very long before Gillian had arrived. She could tell at once that it was a very good neighborhood, nearly as elegant as the area surrounding Meg Fairfax's house. She was somewhat relieved to find such respectable-looking town houses, for after hearing Sir Hewitt so maligned, she had half-expected him to reside in some opulent tawdry palace that might have housed a Turkish sultan. But no, these were sturdy English houses that lined the square, and when she found Number 19, she paused for a moment in front of the walk leading to the house.

Scarcely had she stopped when the door was flung open and a somberly dressed gentleman was thrown bodily outside. "And don't ever come back," shouted a voice from inside. The somberly dressed gentleman was obviously in a rage. He recovered quickly and rushed back toward the door, which was slammed shut in his face, narrowly missing his nose. He cursed and pounded violently upon it.

"Damn you, Gambol," he shouted. "I'll get what's due me. My God, I'll see you in jail, you damned bounder!"

Gillian watched the man continue to pound on the door. There was no response, and so the man muttered an oath, kicked the door hard with his foot, and then turned to leave. Seeing Gillian standing there, he looked embarrassed and, recovering the hat that had been tossed out after him, hastened past her and down the street.

It crossed Gillian's mind that this was hardly a good omen for her first visit with her father. Most young ladies would have retreated swiftly, but Gillian had never been one to give up easily. She had resolved to see Sir Hewitt, and see him she would. It would only be harder to get her courage up if she left now. Taking a deep breath, she proceeded up the short walk to the doorstep and lifted the brass door knocker, allowing it to thud against the door.

She stood there for a while and wondered if anyone

would answer. Then suddenly the door was pulled open. "So you've not had enough, Gregson!"

Gillian gasped. Standing before her was a stout red-faced gentlemen brandishing a cutlass.

"What?" he said. "You ain't Gregson."

Gillian gulped. "No, sir, I am Gillian Ashley."

"Ashley?"

"I am the daughter of Caroline Ashley."

"Good God!"

The red-faced gentleman put down his cutlass and looked somewhat sheepishly at Gillian. "Sorry. Thought it was old Gregson back for more. He's been dunning me for weeks."

"Might I come in, Sir Hewitt? You are Sir Hewitt Gambol, are you not?"

"Can't deny it, it seems. Come in, then, young lady. Caroline's daughter, you say? Damn me I never knew she had a daughter, but you're pretty enough to be. Come in, come in. Moffat! Moffat! Come in here!" Sir Hewitt's shouts brought a grim untidy-looking servant who eyed Gillian suspiciously.

"Take this, you fool," said Sir Hewitt, handing his servant the cutlass. "I've a guest. Fetch us some tea, and be quick about it."

Moffat did not seem at all happy with this pronouncement but went off without a word.

"I'm not used to having callers, miss. Forgive the welcome and come along." He led her into a parlor and instructed her to be seated. She looked around the room, noting its untidiness and the fact that, although it must have once had pretensions to splendor, the room's luxurious furnishings were looking very worn and faded.

Sir Hewitt sat down and grinned at her, and Gillian regarded him with some dismay. So this was her father? He was a round-faced, white-haired satyr with a red nose and stubble on his chin.

"You are Caroline's daughter? How is she?"

"I'm afraid that my mother died nearly a year ago."

Sir Hewitt's face fell. "Dead? Not Caroline?"

Gillian nodded. "She had been ill for some time."

Sir Hewitt stared at her in stricken silence. "Your mother was the finest woman who ever lived. She was a joy, that woman. There was no one who met her who did not love her." He looked suddenly hopeful. "Did she have a message for me?"

Gillian shook her head. "No, I am afraid she did not."

Sir Hewitt looked very disappointed. "She told you about me, then?"

"No, sir. I learned about you from my cousin, Lord Guildford." Gillian paused and took the letter from her reticule. "And this." She handed it to Sir Hewitt. He took it and then fished about in his pocket for his spectacles.

"Damnation, I've lost them. Tell me what it is."

"Allow me to read it to you." She took the paper from him, even though she realized that she knew most of the letter by heart. "My dearest Caroline, I am in agony from your silence. Why won't you answer me? You know I love you above all else and that my life and fortune are yours. My dear, I know how you have suffered, but you are free from Ashley now. I beg you to marry me and allow us to begin life anew. You cannot have forgotten all we were to each other. Stay there and await my arrival. I promise I shall be there soon. I live only to see your face once more. Your adoring and devoted Hewitt."

Sir Hewitt Gambol regarded Gillian strangely. "Why have you come here? Who are you?"

"I am Caroline Ashley's daughter, and it seems, Sir Hewitt, that you are my father."

Oliver Bain entered the home of his oldest friend, John Colville, and handed his hat to the butler. "Is Mr. Colville home?"

"I'm sorry, my lord. Mr. Colville has gone to his club."

"Blast," muttered his lordship, who had been eager to see his best and, some said, only friend.

"But Mrs. Colville is in, my lord. I shall announce you."

"Very well." The earl could scarcely leave without paying his respects to the lady, but he would have rather left to join Mr. Colville at his club.

The butler left and returned shortly. "Do follow me, my lord."

The butler led Bain into an elegant drawing room where Mrs. Colville rose gracefully to welcome him. "My dear Bain, how good of you to come." Mrs. Colville smiled. She was well aware that she was considered one of the great beauties of society. Her face, with its classical features, was acknowledged to be very near perfection, and her figure, which was daringly revealed in the flimsy muslin morning dress she was wearing, was hardly to be surpassed.

The earl, though not unaware of the lady's charms, did not appear impressed. "I cannot stay long, Henrietta. I must join John at the club."

"You men," said Henrietta Colville, pursing her lips in a charming pout. "You are always rushing about with no thought to us ladies. I insist you sit down, Bain. Surely I am not so ugly that I drive you away this quickly."

"You know very well you are the most beautiful woman in London." Bain sat down on the sofa, and although Mrs. Colville was gratified by the compliment, she did not like his lordship's nonchalance and his air of ennui.

She sat down beside him and regarded him with a look that was unabashedly coquettish. She had always thought him the most handsome of her husband's friends. His rugged face, with its rather cynical expression, and his broad shoulders and powerful body had always attracted her, but his seeming indifference exasperated her.

"I so rarely have an opportunity to talk with you, Bain. You have been a stranger too long to this house. Why, only last night John was wondering what had become of you. I believe he intended to call upon you today."

"Then I do hope I can see him at the club."

Afraid that her guest would escape her, Mrs. Colville placed a restraining hand on his arm. "I will not have you running off, Bain. Now tell me what you have been doing." She smiled. "Seeing that it is you, perhaps it is best you do not tell me *all* you have been doing."

Bain felt some irritation at this remark. He had never liked Henriette Colville and had thought his friend John most imprudent in his choice of a wife. It was no secret to anyone except John Colville that his wife had numerous affairs, and she had never been known for her discretion.

"It is being said, Lord Bain, that you have been taking quite an interest in the actress Mrs. Clifford. Really, Bain, she is rather common, is she not?" Henrietta smiled up at him and Bain frowned. She laughed. "Oh, how grim you look. I always told John that you often looked as if you wanted to bite someone. I have told John that you are a very dangerous man. Oh, John does not think so. He thinks you are quite harmless, but I daresay he is the only one."

Mrs. Colville leaned toward the earl and he was made more aware of the low-cut dress she was wearing and the strong scent of her perfume. He could not deny that she was a very attractive woman and the sudden closeness of her made him temporarily forget that she was the wife of his closest friend and a lady whom he disliked heartily.

"You are a handsome fellow, my lord. I have always thought so. I hope you do not find me so very plain." She smiled at him enticingly and he found himself looking from her face to the tantalizing fullness of her breasts. Sensing her opportunity, Mrs. Colville stopped closer to his lordship and, throwing her shoulders back, allowed him an even better view of her considerable charms.

The earl seemed to need no further provocation. He caught Mrs. Colville up into his arms and covered her mouth with his own. Mrs. Colville pressed her body against his, and as he began to cover her neck and breasts with passionate kisses, she moaned with pleasure. "Oh, my dear, my darling. Come upstairs with me. Someone may come in."

Mrs. Colville's throaty whispers seemed to bring Bain to his senses. He pulled away from her. "Good God, what am I doing?"

"Whatever is wrong, my darling?"

Bain took a step back and shook his head. "I am here scarcely five minutes and am about to cuckold my best friend."

"That is a rather unpleasant way of putting it, my dear. Come upstairs with me."

"What sort of man am I? You are John's wife."

"Why must you harp about my husband?" Mrs. Colville was frankly puzzled by Bain's abrupt change.

The earl grinned humorlessly. "And you think so little of deceiving your husband that you would make love to a man you care nothing about? How I pity John, madam."

Mrs. Colville's bewilderment changed rapidly to anger. "How dare you, sir? How dare you? As if your dear John had never been unfaithful to me! And you! You have come by your scruples very recently it seems. Yours is hardly a reputation for virtue. Did you worry so much about the honor of other husbands whose wives you have bedded? Oh, no, but I am John's wife and John is your friend. You are a damned hypocrite, sir, and you may go to the devil!"

This unladylike rebuke was like a slap on the face, and Bain muttered a curt, "Good day, madam," and turned quickly and departed.

He climbed into his awaiting carriage and shouted at his driver to be off. The driver, who had by now become accustomed to his master's very changeable moods, hastened to obey and the carriage made its way through the London streets.

Bain sat in gloomy silence staring at the passing houses. "That damnable woman," he muttered. "Am I so depraved that I leap into her arms at the first opportunity? God in heaven."

He thought suddenly of his mother. She thought him a worthless rake concerned only with his pleasures, and it seemed she was right. Henrietta Colville was right too. He was a damned hypocrite. He had had no qualms about having affairs with a number of bored married ladies. Why was Henrietta so very different just because John was his oldest friend?

Bain thought of his friend and frowned. John Colville did not deserve to be married to such a woman. Henrietta's numerous indiscretions made her husband the object of scorn and pity. It was certainly a black day when he had wed the enchanting and beautiful Henrietta.

Bain thanked Providence again that he had never married. A wife could bring a man down faster than gaming or liquor if one were so foolhardy as to fall in love with her. Poor John had been so in love with Henrietta that he had seen none of her faults; even worse, he loved her still.

The earl was so lost in his grim thoughts that he did not notice where his driver was heading, and when the vehicle stopped, he realized with a start that he had arrived at his club. "Damn your eyes, Harry," he shouted. "I didn't tell you to go here." The driver was quite dismayed, for, since his employer had given him no other instructions, he had assumed he wanted to go to his club.

"Oliver? What luck!"

Bain looked out his carriage window and saw John Colville standing in front of the club.

"I say, I cannot believe my good fortune. I was just

leaving and whom do I see pull up but the illustrious Earl of Bain. You are a welcome sight, old boy. I don't suppose you might give me a lift home?"

"Get in, John."

"I'm not sure if I should. It seems you're in a devil of a mood. Something wrong?"

"Not a thing, but I'd rather we didn't hold our conversation on the street corner, if you please, John."

John Colville climbed into the carriage and sat opposite Bain. "What is the matter, Oliver?"

"I should rather not discuss it," snapped his lordship, and his friend studied him carefully. There was obviously something troubling the earl, but Colville knew better than to press Bain when he was in one of his moods.

They rode in silence and soon arrived at the Colville house. "Won't you come in, Oliver? Henrietta would like to see you."

"I called earlier and have already seen your wife. I will not burden her with another visit."

"Very well, Oliver." John Colville decided to give up. He would be very happy to listen if Bain wished to confide in him, but he had no more patience left. "Good day, then. Perhaps I shall see you at the club tomorrow."

Bain nodded. "Yes, I shall be there."

Colville started to get out of the carraige.

"John?"

Colville hesitated. "What is it?"

"I am sorry I'm such poor company."

Colville smiled. "That's all right, old man." He got out of the carriage and watched it pull off. "Poor old Bain," he muttered, and walked briskly up the walk to join his wife.

Sir Hewitt Gambol stared uncomprehensively at Gillian. "Father? I your father?"

Gillian nodded.

"I, a father? By the great hound, I cannot believe it!"

"I know it is a great shock to you, sir, and I did not wish to upset you, but I have only just now become aware of the fact myself. I never knew until very recently."

Sir Hewitt did not seem to be listening. His florid countenance bore a very perplexed expression and he kept muttering, "I, a father?" He finally looked closely at Gillian, squinting as he did so, for he was extremely shortsighted. "Damn me if there ain't a trace of Hewitt blood. Shows about the eyes and the nose too. Dashed pretty girl you are, but by God, all the Hewitt women were beauties in their day." Sir Hewitt gestured toward an enormous painting that hung in a gilt frame. "My grandmother. Damn me if you don't look like her."

Gillian studied the features of the lady in the portrait and was not sure if she liked the idea of resembling her. She was a very stern-looking woman in a powdered wig with rather prominent front teeth, and she scowled menacingly down at her posterity.

"Caroline and myself? By God, you are our daughter?"

"You do not deny it is a possibility."

Sir Hewitt looked thoughtful. "It is a damned good possibility now that I think about it." The elderly gentleman looked suddenly embarrassed. "Your pardon, I had best watch what I say. I don't mean to shock you."

Gillian, who was not in the least shocked, was growing concerned for Sir Hewitt's health. "You are overtiring yourself, sir. Won't you sit down?"

"Sit down? Yes, yes, that would be in order."

Gillian assisted him to the sofa and sat down beside him. "Would you like me to get you a glass of water?"

"Water? Don't drink it myself, but I could use a sherry."

Gillian espied the carafe on the sideboard and hurried to fetch her father a glass. He swallowed it quickly and gratefully. "And now, what, miss?"

"Now, what? Oh, of course, I expect you wonder what I am here for. I have come to ask your assistance, but rest assured I do not intend to try to take your fortune from you. You see, I am currently staying with Lady Meg Fairfax, a very kind lady—"

"And a fine-looking one," Sir Hewitt interjected.

"Lady Fairfax is allowing me to stay with her, which is so generous, especially when you understand I came to her a complete stranger without so much as an introduction. She would like to introduce me into society, although I keep telling her that it will not do, she will not take no for an answer. But I have no ambitions in society, Sir Hewitt. I only wish to be able to support myself and be a burden on no one. I have told Lady Meg that I wish to obtain a position as a governess, and although she does not think it a good idea, I can think of nothing else I am suited for. What I ask of you, sir, is to lend me a small amount to live on until I am able to find a position."

Sir Hewitt put down the glass and regarded Gillian curiously. "You want to be a governess?"

"It would not be so bad an existence."

Sir Hewitt shook his head. "No daughter of mine will be a servant to anyone."

"Governess. It is quite respectable."

"Hang it, miss, I won't hear of it! I'll not sully the family name by assisting you in this. My daughter a governess? What would Caroline say?"

Gillian suppressed a smile and thought it odd that Sir Hewitt would speak of sullying the family name. "I must be realistic, Sir Hewitt. My background does not make me a very desirable young lady in society's highest circles."

"Your background? You are the daughter of Sir Hewitt Gambol, baronet and gentleman. There is no older family in all of England."

"But do not forget I am not your daughter in the legal sense."

"But you are my daughter, and by God you'll take your rightful place in society."

"Please do not upset yourself." Gillian smiled at Sir Hewitt. "It seems, sir, that you are taking this surprisingly well. I think many men would have tossed me from their doorstep."

"You've Hewitt blood, I can see that plainly now."

"Then you don't mind?"

"Mind? Damn me if I ain't overjoyed. I'm alone now. There's no one left of the family. Of course, I never married. No point in it, after Caroline. I've not always been such a virtuous fellow . . ."

Gillian smiled at his understatement.

"A man starts to think about his life when he gets on in years. I've not done much good in this life, but you, my girl, I can tell you're a lady, like your mother. Damn me if this ain't the best news to come to me in years. I, a father!" Sir Hewitt grinned. "Do you think . . . No, I suppose not."

"What is it?"

Sir Hewitt laughed sheepish. "Could you call me Papa?"

Gillian laughed and took his hand. "I don't see why not . . . Papa."

Sir Hewitt laughed delightedly and pressed her hand.

six

Two well-dressed young gentlemen strolled down the street. They had both taken considerable trouble with their appearance, for they were dandies of the first order and were most anxious to make a favorable impression on whomever they happened to pass on this fashionable London street.

"I say, Fanshawe, look at that!" One of the young gentlemen stopped short.

"Good heavens," said his companion, "Hewitt Gambol!"

The two men watched with great interest as Sir Hewitt and Gillian walked slowly down the front steps of his house. Sir Hewitt leaned on his cane and took Gillian's arm for support. They made their way into an awaiting carriage and, much to the two young observers' disappointment, vanished from sight.

"Did you get a look at that girl, Thornbury? She was a fine-looking thing."

"I saw her well enough. But Gambol? By God, I had thought him at death's door and now he appears with a new bit of muslin at his side. One must admire the fellow's fortitude."

"And his choice of women. Poor girl must be in a bad way to take up with him."

"My dear Fanshawe, I do not doubt that she is indeed. You cannot expect her to be an heiress, now can you? But I cannot wait to tell my sister. She was just the other day saying that old Gambol was finally getting what he deserved. She'll be so very upset to find there's life in the old boy still."

Fanshawe grinned. "It seems there is life indeed."

Meg Fairfax awakened from her nap feeling quite refreshed and happy that her headache had disappeared. She descended the stairs and entered the library, but was surprised to see it empty. She had assumed Gillian Ashley would be there reading.

"Oh, Hull," she said, addressing the butler, "where is Miss Ashley?"

"Miss has gone out, my lady," came the reply.

"Out?"

"Some time ago, my lady. She did not say where she was going."

"Very good, Hull," muttered Lady Fairfax, quite perplexed. Where had Gillian gone? It would never do for her to be out wandering about town without so much as informing the servants where she was off to.

Lady Fairfax retired to the drawing room and took up her embroidery. She had no sooner begun work when she heard someone at the door. Moments later in came Gillian. On her arm was a stout elderly man with a very red face, whom Meg recognized to her horror as Sir Hewitt Gambol. It was a credit to Lady Meg's impeccable breeding that she did not gape in astonishment, but managed a very civil and seemingly unperturbed greeting.

"So there you are, Gillian."

"I am sorry to have run off without leaving word, Meg, but I had to see him, and here he is. Lady Fairfax, may I present Sir Hewitt Gambol, my father."

Sir Hewitt smiled a satyrlike grin and bowed grandly. "Charmed, ma'am."

"How do you do." Meg tried to hide her revulsion. How could Gillian have been so thoughtless to have brought the man here? What if someone had seen him arrive?

Gillian seemed unconcerned about the social consequences of bringing the notorious Sir Hewitt into Lady Fairfax's drawing room. She assisted Sir Hewitt to be seated on the sofa across from Meg and sat down beside him.

"He took it very well, Meg. It was a shock, though, was it not, Papa?"

Meg cringed to hear Gillian call the dissolute Sir Hewitt Papa. He smiled delightedly and patted Gillian's hand. "Damn me, Lady Fairfax, if this ain't a great day for me. You might have knocked me over to hear it at first. You can imagine what it is like to have a little lady like Gillian come up to your door and announce she is your daughter. God in heaven, I was bowled over for a bit, seeing how much she looks like my grandmother and damn me if there ain't quite a bit of me in that pretty little face. Not that you can see it so much now, but 'tis there plain as day to me."

Meg looked from Gillian's lovely face to Sir Hewitt's bloated countenance and thought, She's not one whit like you, you old gargoyle. She said, however, "I am gratified you took the news so well."

"He is really marvelous about it." Gillian smiled affectionately at Sir Hewitt, and Meg felt disgusted.

"And I am to do right by her. She'll have my fortune when I'm gone."

"Papa, I don't wish to hear such talk. You've only just met me. I have told you I don't want your fortune, just a small amount of assistance."

"Do you hear that, Lady Fairfax? Ain't she a fine one?

You can tell she's got Hewitt blood well enough. But let us get down to business, eh, madam?"

"Get down to business, Sir Hewitt?"

"Aye, ma'am. The girl has said you've been helping her and I'm right grateful. She says you wish to help her come out into society."

"Papa—"

"No, let me speak, my dear. Lady Fairfax, I expect you've heard her spout that nonsense about becoming a governess. Well, I won't hear of it. No, my girl, you are my daughter and a lady. You must take your rightful place in society. Now, I have considered the matter, and knowing Lady Fairfax to be a respectable lady and fit companion . . ."

"How generous of you to say so," said Meg with an ironic smile.

"If you are willing to aid Gillian, I shall pay all her expenses."

"Papa—"

"No, let me speak. I shall pay for all the gowns and jewels and other fripperies girls need. I shall be extremely grateful to you if you will take Gillian under your wing."

"I shall be only too happy to do so, Sir Hewitt."

"But Meg—"

"I will not hear a word from you, Gillian," Meg said sternly. She turned to Sir Hewitt. "I think you are being quite fair and responsible. I shall see that Gillian gets all the things she needs."

"And do not spare the expense."

"Very well, we shall not."

"I want my girl to have the best."

Meg Fairfax hesitated for a moment and then decided she had best say what was on her mind. "There is something, Sir Hewitt, that I must insist upon. I am happy to help Gillian. You see what a charming young lady she is, but I must be blunt, sir. If you wish her to have all the advantages, you must disassociate yourself from her as much as possible."

"Meg!"

"I said I would be blunt. In short, sir, your reputation is such that any connection between yourself and Gillian would be a distinct disadvantage to her."

Gillian looked at Sir Hewitt, fearing that his feelings would be quite hurt and that he would be sorely offended. However, Sir Hewitt only laughed. "You're not one to mince words, are you, ma'am? You're right. I know it. I'll not come near Gillian. I don't want to spoil things."

"Well, no one shall stop me from seeing you. You are my father and the only family I have in the entire world. I do not care what anyone thinks, especially those stuffy old society people."

"Spoken like a true Gambol! I want you to be a fine lady, minx, and you'll not ruin your chances by hanging about an old roué like me. Listen to Lady Fairfax. She knows what's best."

Meg was relieved by Sir Hewitt's common sense and decided to venture to offer him tea. She was not disappointed when he refused and rose to go. Gillian helped him make his way out of the house, down the stairs, and into the awaiting carriage, and after bestowing a dutiful kiss on his red cheek, Gillian waved to him as he went off.

"Isn't he the kindest man?" Gillian said as she reentered the drawing room.

"He is not universally regarded as such, but you seem to have charmed him. And he you, though God knows why. But I am grateful to him for helping you to see the wisdom of my plan. Now, I am not going to hear any more from you about this silly governess business. You cannot refuse your father's aid."

"No, I suppose I cannot," said Gillian.

"Good. Now that that is settled, let us retire to my rooms. There is the Bickerstaff party coming up and I think you would look very lovely in my pearls. No, I will not hear any protests. Come along.''

Gillian smiled gratefully at her ladyship and followed her from the room.

seven

T he Earl of Bain arrived at his cousin's house early the next afternoon only to find that Lady Fairfax was not at home. However, the butler informed him that Miss Ashley had not accompanied her ladyship and was in the library.

When the earl was ushered into the library, he found Gillian propped in the window seat, a book in her lap. As he entered, she smiled and seemed genuinely glad to see him.

"Lord Bain, how good of you to call."

His lordship returned her smile and glanced at the book on her lap. "Good day, Miss Ashley. It appears I have disturbed your reading."

"That is quite all right. It is a rather tragic tale and I am very glad to put it down." Gillian rose from the window seat. "Do sit down, Lord Bain. I am eager to tell you all about my visit to my father."

"Your father? You don't mean Sir Hewitt Gambol?"

"I do indeed." She sat down in one of the room's very comfortable chairs and Bain sat down on the sofa across from her.

"Don't tell me that my cousin agreed to take you there."

"Not exactly. You see, I went there on my own without

telling Lady Fairfax. But it worked out very well. Sir Hewitt took the news so well. I think he was happy to find he has a daughter, but then I suspect he is rather lonely. And he is the sweetest man.''

Bain's eyebrows arched in disbelief. "Are you sure you actually met Sir Hewitt?"

"My lord! You must take care about insulting my father. I don't care what anyone may say about him, he was very nice to me. And he would not hear of my becoming a governess. He thought Lady Fairfax's idea to bring me out in society a good one, and he will pay all my expenses." Gillian looked over at Bain. "I am not so sure it is a good idea, but it seems I am destined to attempt it."

"I shouldn't worry about it. I think you'll do very well. And with my cousin's aid, you shall be wed in no time."

"You're mocking me, Lord Bain."

"No," he said, "I'm completely serious." He changed the subject abruptly. "It is a fine spring day. I thought you and Meg might enjoy a ride in the park. Where is my cousin, by the way?"

"Oh, she went to pay a call on Lady Carlisle." Gillian smiled somewhat sheepishly. "Meg wanted me to accompany her, but I begged off. I am glad I did, for I would love to go for a ride in the park."

To her surprise the earl hesitated.

"Is something wrong, sir?"

Bain looked at her perplexed expression and smiled. He had just been wondering what people would think if he were seen squiring Gillian Ashley about the town unchaperoned. The earl was quite aware of his reputation and did not think it would be to the lady's advantage to be seen alone with him.

"I don't think it would be a good idea for you to be seen with me unchaperoned."

"Do you fear for your reputation, my lord?"

The earl laughed. "It is your reputation I am thinking of, Miss Ashley."

"What nonsense, Lord Bain! Have you forgotten who I am? I am certain that most of society would be scandalized just knowing of my existence."

"Then you must take special caution with your behavior . . . and whom you are seen with. You don't wish to confirm any mistaken opinions."

The earl's tone sounded very much like a schoolmaster lecturing his pupil, and Gillian burst out in exasperation. "Oh, don't be such a . . . such a . . . puritan!"

The Earl of Bain stared at her for a moment and then burst into laughter.

Gillian smiled. "I see, my lord, that few have accused you of that before. You do not seem so very wicked to me."

His lordship paused, and when he replied, it was in a serious voice. "I have not led an exemplary life, Miss Ashley. I have done few things of which I may be proud."

Gillian shook her head. "I cannot believe that, my lord. Do you forget how you saved me from that odious footpad?"

The earl smiled. "I had rather thought, madam, that you had saved yourself from the fellow."

"And then you took me to Meg. It was very kind of you. Indeed, you are a very good and kind gentleman. So do not think you can convince me that you are some kind of blackguard, because I know differently. And as for what society thinks of me, I don't care one whit."

The earl shook his head. "I can see there is no point in arguing with you. After all, you are a young lady who considers Sir Hewitt Gambol 'sweet.' "

"Then perhaps we should go for a ride?" Gillian said.

"Oh, very well."

Gillian laughed. "Just let me get my bonnet. I won't be but a moment."

True to her word, Gillian returned very shortly and they left the house. Gillian was quite impressed when they got inside and she saw the earl's high-perch phaeton and team of four bay horses. "What magnificent horses," she said.

The earl smiled and deftly lifted her up into the phaeton. He then climbed up beside her, and taking the reins from his groom, he urged the horses into a sedate trot.

Gillian had never ridden in a high-perch phaeton before and she was quite thrilled at finding herself regarding the streets of London from such a lofty position. As they drove along, the earl pointed out several historical landmarks and was amused by Gillian's enthusiasm for the ancient statues and buildings that most Londoners passed every day without giving them a thought.

They came to the park and the earl urged the horses into a faster pace. Gillian watched the earl with admiration as he skillfully overtook a sluggish carriage in front of them. The earl had made the maneuver look quite easy.

"You are quite a hand with the ribbons, my lord," said Gillian.

Bain acknowledged the compliment with a slight smile.

"How I envy you," Gillian continued wistfully. "I should like nothing better than dashing about in my own phaeton." She looked over at the earl, and a thought suddenly struck her. "Lord Bain . . . do you think . . . would you possibly . . . ?"

The Earl of Bain gave her an amused sidelong glance. "I shouldn't be able to tell you, Miss Ashley, unless you finish your sentence."

Gillian smiled and quickly blurted out, "Would you show me how to drive?"

Gillian was surprised at how the earl's smiling face suddenly turned to a mask of stone. "I'm afraid not, Miss Ashley."

"But I assure you I would not do anything foolish, my lord. Please show me."

"No," said the earl brusquely, and Gillian was suddenly annoyed.

"Is it because I'm a woman, sir?" she asked indignantly. "I have seen other ladies driving about. Why, Lady McNeil in Edinburgh used to drive about town in a six-in-hand. And I daresay she could out race any gentleman in Edinburgh."

"I don't care if Lady McNeil could out race the devil," muttered his lordship.

Gillian, who was quite surprised at the earl's reaction to her request, looked insulted. "There is no need for you to be so unpleasant. I am very sorry I asked. I shan't do so again, I assure you."

They rode in silence for a time, Bain regretting the vehemence of his reaction and Gillian wondering if she had misjudged his lordship. She had assumed he would not object to her taking the reins for a short distance and was sorely disappointed.

Bain slowed his horses as they neared the end of the park. "Would you like to go somewhere else, or are you so upset with me that you would prefer to go home?"

"I am not really upset with you, my lord, and if you are not so eager to be rid of me, I should like to go on."

"Good." Bain seemed quite amiable now. "Is there any place in particular you would like to go?" he said.

"There is one place—two, actually. But you would think it silly."

"Tell me."

"I should like to see Westminster Abbey and the Tower. Oh, I knew you would think it silly."

Bain grinned. "I do not think it in the least silly, and if you wish to see Westminster Abbey and the Tower, Miss Ashley, we shall hasten in that direction."

Their friendly relationship restored, Gillian and Bain talked of many subjects. It seemed to his lordship that the congested drive to Westminster Abbey did not take nearly so long as he had supposed.

Bain was amused by Gillian's awe at entering Westminster Abbey. Her blue eyes opened wide and she seemed genuinely affected by the magnificence of the cathedral. An elderly church deacon, seeing them enter and judging that they were persons of consequence, hastened to offer his services as guide.

Gillian was delighted and Bain could only nod in agreement, although he dreaded the long-winded lectures such churchmen were known to give. Much to Bain's surprise, he found he began to enjoy the tour and the deacon's rambling discourse on Gothic architecture and history. Gillian seemed so fascinated that his lordship started to take a new interest in the somber effigy figures of knights and their ladies. They paused long at the tomb of Queen Elizabeth and longer still at the tomb of the unfortunate Mary, Queen of Scots.

When at last the tour had ended and the earl had given the deacon a generous contribution for the cathedral fund, they emerged from the medieval past into bright sunlight.

"Wasn't that the most wonderful visit? Oh, Lord Bain, I do thank you for taking me. I do hope you weren't bored."

"Bored? How could I be bored with the fellow's vivid description of poor Mary's beheading?"

Gillian laughed. "He did seem rather interested in executions, did he not? Do you think there is enough time to see the Tower?"

"So you haven't heard enough of executions for one day, miss? Well, if I can locate my man with the carriage, I imagine we have time for a visit." Bain looked along the street for his phaeton and espying it, turned to Gillian. "There it is."

Gillian, however, had seen something else of interest.

"Oh, look," she said. "Do you see the poor woman over there? What do you think is the matter?"

Bain followed Gillian's gaze to a very large woman in shabby clothes who was clutching a little boy by the hand and sobbing into her handkerchief.

"I'm sure I don't know. But Harry has seen us and is bringing the carriage round. Come along, miss. It is some distance to the Tower."

"I think there is something wrong. I think I shall see if we can help her."

"Wait just a moment," said his lordship, eyeing the sobbing woman with disapproval. "She doesn't look like the sort you should speak to. She is doubtless upset over some trivial matter. You know how women are." The earl knew as soon as the words escaped him that he had said the wrong thing.

Gillian regarded him with indignation. "You men," she said. "Well, I do not care what you do, sir, but I am going to see what is the matter with the poor woman." Gillian walked resolutely away and his lordship could only follow.

"Is there something I could do to assist you, madam?" Gillian spoke to the sobbing woman, who looked at her with an expression akin to astonishment. She stopped crying and dabbed her eyes with her handkerchief.

"How good of you to ask, miss," she said, "how very good of you."

The earl was regarding the woman with disfavor, noting her disheveled appearance and that the little boy at her side was decidedly dirty and in his lordship's view a most unappealing creature. Seeming to sense the gentleman's disapproval, the little boy broke into tears and buried his head against the woman's skirt.

"Now, now, Alfred, stop your crying. The lady and gentleman want to help your old ma, 'tis all."

"If you would tell me what is wrong, perhaps we could help."

"That is good of you, miss. I don't wish to trouble you."

At this remark, the earl was about to say "good" and forcefully drag Gillian away, but the sobbing woman continued. "I come in from Putney this morning to visit my sister Daisy. We usually have such nice visits, her being so nicely settled. Married to a butcher, she is, and doing right well for herself."

Bain was listening to this with increasing annoyance and a sense of incredulity that the illustrious Earl of Bain would find himself enduring such a conversation.

"We quarreled, you see, miss. Oh, not Daisy and me, but that sister-in-law of hers. My, that woman takes on airs. I never could abide her. Well, I wasn't about to take any talk from the like o' her, so I take little Alfred and off I go. Mr. Webb, that is my sister's husband, was to see us home as he always does. He knows a fellow owns a wagon what drives to Putney every Tuesday and that is how we get back, but we run off and have walked for miles and I don't have any money to get home and don't know how to get there even if I did, and poor Alfred's so tired." The woman began to cry again and little Alfred started to wail.

"Good God," muttered his lordship.

"Don't worry, Mrs.—oh, I don't know your name."

"Mrs. Rumstead, miss."

"Don't worry, Mrs. Rumstead. We shall see you get home."

The earl started to pull a coin from his pocket, for he was eager for Mrs. Rumstead and her son to cease their din. "His lordship has a carriage waiting and we shall be glad to take you to Putney."

The earl stared at Gillian in disbelief. "Surely, Miss Ashley, the lady would prefer to take some public conveyance."

Mrs. Rumstead did not seem to hear his comment but had certainly heard "his lordship."

"His lordship?" Mrs. Rumstead gasped and made a ludicrous curtsy. "Oh, if your lordship would be so kind, I should be so proud. You are a saint, my lord, a gentleman like your lordship offering to help a poor woman like myself."

"There is the carriage," Gillian said, taking Mrs. Rumstead by the arm. "Do come along."

Little Alfred, after perceiving that he was to ride in a fancy carriage, stopped crying immediately. He loosened his grip on his mother's hand and raced to the carriage, where the earl's groom was studying the Rumsteads with great interest. Bain was frowning ominously. Was it possible that he was about to escort this woman and her brat to Putney?

"Such good Christian folk you are," babbled Mrs. Rumstead, elated at the prospect of riding in a carriage with a bona fide lordship and a lovely lady of fashion. The earl winced as his groom helped Mrs. Rumstead into his phaeton and wondered at the effect her considerable bulk would have on his vehicle's springs. Little Alfred jumped into the carriage and bounced up and down on the upholstered seat.

"Mind your manners, Alfred," scolded Mrs. Rumstead, and the little boy reluctantly settled down.

Bain gave Gillian a grim look as he handed her into the carriage, but the young lady did not seem to notice it. She began to chat with Mrs. Rumstead in a manner the earl thought very familiar and ill-advised. His lordship knew well the dangers of familiarity with one's inferiors.

The earl's groom leapt agilely into the driver's seat and waited for his master's instructions. "Putney," said Bain ill-humoredly.

"Putney, my lord?"

"That is what I said, Harry, and make good speed."

They started off and Bain silently cursed the congested London streets and Gillian's rash charity. He looked daggers at Mrs. Rumstead, who with Gillian was sitting across from him. Seated beside him was little Alfred, who was enjoying himself immensely.

Alfred grinned up at the earl and ventured to speak. "They are pretty horses, sir."

Bain regarded the little boy coldly, but even he could not be unaffected by the child, who was, despite his untidyness, a charming little boy. "Thank you."

"You must say 'my lord,' Alfred. The gentleman is a lord." Mrs. Rumstead hastened to correct her son.

Alfred looked up at the earl, obviously impressed. "Are you like the king?"

Gillian burst into laughter, and Bain, despite his black mood, found himself smiling.

"Alfred," admonished Mrs. Rumstead, "do not plague his lordship with questions. Ride quietly."

Alfred obeyed and turned his attention to watching the horses and Lord Bain. He seemed to find his lordship as fascinating as the horses and stared up at him from time to time.

Mrs. Rumstead, although proclaiming that she was quite overwhelmed to be in such illustrious company and in such a beautiful carriage, soon was very much at ease. She chattered away, hardly allowing Gillian to get a word in. Bain was irritated to find that Gillian seemed to be enjoying Mrs. Rumstead's company, laughing at her remarks and encouraging her to act in a manner far above her station.

When the carriage stopped for traffic at the intersection of two busy streets at the western edge of the city, another carriage pulled along side and Bain found himself raising his hat to the other vehicle's occupants, the Duke and Duchess of Welbourne.

His lordship knew that the duchess would waste no time informing all of her acquaintances of the Earl of Bain's unusual traveling companions. Bain scowled as the other carriage pulled away.

"My, those were very grand personages," Mrs. Rumstead said, hoping his lordship would enlighten her as to the identity of the lady and gentleman. When no comment was forthcoming, Gillian looked over at Bain.

"Was that the Duchess of Welbourne? Lady Fairfax pointed her out to me when we were shopping."

"A duchess? My goodness," said Mrs. Rumstead.

Bain said nothing but folded his arms across his chest and looked blackly at both of them. Little Alfred, who was watching his lordship's every move, folded his arms across his chest and then studied the earl to be sure that he was doing it correctly.

After what seemed a very long time to Lord Bain, they arrived at Putney and the street where Mrs. Rumstead's modest little house was located. Unlike Bain, Mrs. Rumstead was not eager to end her adventure. "I don't suppose you would condescend to have tea with me?"

"You are kind," said the earl quickly before Gillian could speak, "but Miss Ashley and myself are due back in town. We haven't much time. Harry, assist Mrs. Rumstead down."

The earl then suffered Mrs. Rumstead's expressions of gratitude and her awkward curtsy and was forced to shake little Alfred's rather sticky hand.

As they drove away from the Rumstead house, Bain looked darkly at Gillian.

"I daresay, my lord," remarked Gillian, seemingly unaware of her danger, "you might have been a bit more gracious. Surely we had enough time to have tea. Mrs. Rumstead was a very amusing woman, don't you think?"

"Indeed. I hope you have left her your calling card and invited her to visit you and Meg."

Gillian noted the sarcasm in his voice and looked up into his brown eyes. "Why, you are angry."

"Does that surprise you? God in heaven, I am not accustomed to providing every common woman I see on the street with a ride home to Putney. Have you no sense of propriety? I was quite willing to give the awful woman money to find her way home, but no, you had to be the Good Samaritan.''

"I did not think it so great a chore to take her home."

"By God, it was a chore to endure her coarse vulgar prattle. And then we were seen by the Duke and Duchess of Welbourne. I shall be laughed out of my club.''

"I didn't know you were so concerned about society's opinion of you.''

"Dammit, don't you understand what a stupid thing you have done?''

Gillian blinked in surprise. "Stupid?''

"Have you no regard for your position? A lady does not ride about with such persons, treating them as equals. You will give the woman ideas far above her station and cause nothing but harm.''

"So now you are worried about Mrs. Rumstead? Egad, you are such a snob. I have misjudged you, Lord Bain. It seems you are concerned only with your own self-importance.''

Bain glared at Gillian, thinking her the most exasperating female he had ever met.

"Harry,'' he shouted to his servant, "make haste to Lady Fairfax's house. Hurry, damn you!''

Gillian frowned. They did not say another word to each other the rest of the way.

"My dear Gillian, whatever happened between you and Bain?'' Meg Fairfax had been quite alarmed when her cousin and Gillian had entered her house, both of them looking in the foulest of moods. Bain had said scarcely a word and had left hurriedly, and Meg was quite perplexed. She led Gillian over to the drawing-room sofa. "I want to hear what happened. It seems something has caused my cousin's famous temper to flare up.''

"Oh, Meg, I vexed him, it seems. I had no idea he would react so badly. Oh, I suppose I was more concerned with Mrs. Rumstead, but I had no idea he so resented helping her."

"My dear, I do not have the least idea about what you are talking about. Who is Mrs. Rumstead?"

"A woman we met outside Westminster Abbey. You know, Meg, I did not realize what a difficult man your cousin is." Gillian went on to describe Mrs. Rumstead and little Alfred, and as soon as she told how she had offered to take them home, Meg erupted into gales of laughter.

"You didn't! What did Bain say?"

"I guess I didn't give him the opportunity to say anything. Oh, dear, I was a bit foward, it seems. But poor Mrs. Rumstead was so distraught."

"Oh, I wish I could have seen Bain's face!"

"He was very perturbed when we were seen by the Duchess of Welbourne."

Meg burst into renewed laughter. "Oh, that *is* funny. I cannot imagine what that awful woman must have thought to see this Mrs. Rumstead. Poor Bain. You must understand he has such pride and does not travel about in his beloved phaeton with just anyone."

"I think he is too concerned about things like carriages. Why, even before we met Mrs. Rumstead, he made it very clear that only he could be trusted to drive his carriage."

Meg Fairfax grew suddenly serious. "What do you mean?"

"We were riding through the park and I asked if I might take the reins for a moment, just to see what it was like and he nearly bit my head off."

"Oh, dear."

"What is it, Meg?"

"You see, Gillian, there is something you must know about Oliver. It concerns an accident that happened three years ago. You see, he has always been a great sportsman and no one can touch him at the ribbons. When he was young, he was thought to be quite reckless, forever racing about, indifferent to danger.

"His brother Edgar was not at all like that. I suspect Edgar envied his younger brother's ability with horses. Anyway, three years ago there was a tragic accident. Oliver had a new curricle and some horses that were the talk of the town. It seems they were very spirited animals, and Oliver did not trust anyone but himself to handle them.

"Edgar asked if he might take the curricle out to try the horses, and Oliver refused. He did not think Edgar capable of controlling them. Anyway, there was something of a row and finally Oliver gave in. Edgar was still angry when he took the horses out. He ignored all of Oliver's pleas to be careful. It seems he was eager to show his brother that he was as good a whip as he." Meg paused. "He lost control of the horses and was thrown from the curricle. He was killed instantly.

"Oliver then succeeded him as Earl of Bain. He has never forgiven himself for allowing Edgar to take the horses. So you must understand, Gillian, how he would react when you asked him to take the reins."

"Oh, Meg, if only I had known."

"You cannot be expected to know about it. Indeed, I know he would be quite upset that I told you about it. But I do want you to understand what was behind his reaction. But let us not dwell on the matter. In three days' time is Lady Bickerstaff's ball. It is the perfect occasion for your introduction to society."

Gillian nodded and for Meg's benefit tried to appear excited at the prospect. However, she was not really thinking about the forthcoming ball, but about the Earl of Bain.

eight

"Och, miss, ye look beautiful!" Mary Mac-
Donald had just finished fastening the clasp
on Gillian's borrowed pearls and stood back to admire her
handiwork.

"Stuff and nonsense, Mary," laughed Gillian, staring at
her reflection in the glass. "Well, I do admit I look well
enough. You have done wonders with my hair. Thank
you."

"Will ye be needing anything else, miss?"

"No, Mary. Why don't you be off and see if her ladyship needs anything?"

"Very well, miss." Mary MacDonald left Gillian sitting
at the dressing table reflecting on her changed circumstances. She fingered the string of pearls around her neck.
They were very beautiful and she did not doubt that they
were worth a fortune. She hoped that nothing would
happen to them and almost wished she were wearing some
less expensive adornment. Still, they looked very well with
the blue gauze gown that had been so expertly fashioned by
Madame Bonacieux.

Gillian studied her elaborate coiffure in the mirror and
wondered how Mary had ever arranged her dark tresses so
expertly. A blue plume had been somehow attached, and
although Gillian was briefly reminded of a horse she had

once seen in a circus, she thought the plume looked very elegant.

"Are you ready, Gillian?" Meg Fairfax entered her room and Gillian stood up from the dressing table.

"Oh, Meg, you look wonderful."

Meg Fairfax cast a quick glance down at her gown of rose-colored satin. "It is nice, isn't it? I do think the color suits me. But, my dear, it is you who look wonderful. I must be mad to attach myself to someone like you. Beside you, I look perfectly dowdy."

"You look beautiful."

"Oh, very well, we both look beautiful. I daresay there will not be a male eye turned our way in admiration and a female eye turned our way in envious rage."

Gillian laughed. "Thank you so much for everything, Meg, and for allowing me to wear the pearls."

"Ah, how well they look on you. I see I was right, but then I am a very good judge of such things. Well, come along then, my dear, our carriage awaits."

"I do hope it will go well."

"You are not nervous, are you?"

"Indeed I am. Mary said the prince may be there."

"Mary chatters too much. Yes, I expect Prinny will attend. It is Lady Bickerstaff's ball and she is one of Lady Hertford's closest friends. And of course, you know about Lady Hertford."

"But I do not."

"My poor dear. I daresay Edinburgh is a very long way away. Lady Hertford is His Royal Highness's latest amour."

"But I thought he was in love with Mrs. Fitzherbert."

"Oh, my, that is very much over. Goodness, I see I should have spent some time filling you in on who is who and what is what. There just hasn't been enough time. But you can be sure that Prinny will attend with Lady Hertford on his arm."

"What if he should speak to me? I might die of fright."

"My dear Gillian, from what I have seen of you I doubt you would die of fright were you to be surrounded by savage hordes. If Prinny should condescend to speak to you, it is a very great honor. Take care to say nothing witty to him. HRH finds wit suspect in a woman. But do not worry, I doubt if you will get very close to the prince. It is always so hard to get near him surrounded as he is by the great crowd of sycophants and flatterers. But, my dear, we had best be off. We do not dare to be late, for we risk arriving just as Prinny does and, my dear, that would never do. Prinny must be the last to arrive."

Gillian regarded Meg with a puzzled look and thought that court etiquette must be rather confusing. Meg did not take time to explain further but made her charge snatch up her wrap. They were going to the ball.

Lady Bickerstaff's magnificent London house was as fine an example of Restoration architecture as could be found anywhere. Its elegant and spacious interior was filled with some of the leaders of society, all of them dressed in their finest. The ladies glittered with jewels and the gentlemen exuded power and privilege. In short, it was the sort of gathering that most hostesses could only dream about.

Among the guests was Lady Cavendish. She stood beside another very well-dressed lady and three distinguished-looking gentlemen. "And you cannot imagine my astonishment," Lady Cavendish was saying, "to find that the young lady's name is Miss Gillian Ashley."

"You mean some relation of Lady Honoria Ashley and Christobel Stourbridge?" said one of the gentlemen.

"That is a debatable point, Harlan. The young lady in question is none other than the child of Caroline Ashley. You must remember the *grand scandale* some twenty years back. We talked of nothing else for weeks."

"Good heavens, then this is the daughter of Sir Hewitt

Gambol? He was the one named in the divorce. I shall never forget the duel between him and Rowland Ashley."

Lady Cavendish nodded. "And now the girl is being taken about town by Meg Fairfax. What interest she can have in the girl is quite a mystery to me. I would not be surprised if she turns up here."

"Do you think so, Lady Cavendish?" The other lady seemed quite delighted by the prospect. "I should love to see her. And I should love to see Christobel Stourbridge's face when this Miss Ashley appears."

The ladies and gentlemen laughed. "Hewitt Gambol's daughter?" said one of the gentlemen. "I can imagine what she must look like."

A young man stopped beside the group. "Pardon me for interrupting but did I hear the name Hewitt Gambol?"

"Really, Thornbury, are you eavesdropping?"

"My dear Lady Cavendish, of course."

They all laughed. "I heard the name mentioned and I thought I must see what it is about. You see, I just saw Sir Hewitt the other day and you should have seen the pretty little thing he had on his arm. Can you imagine? And he looked quite awful, very near death's door I should think."

Before any of the others could comment, two new arrivals were announced and the people assembled by Lady Cavendish watched with keen interest as Meg Fairfax and Gillian entered the room.

"Good God!" said the young man named Thornbury. "That looks very much like the girl who was with Gambol. Who would think a creature like her would take up with him?"

"My poor Thornbury," Lady Cavendish said, relishing the reaction she knew her statement would cause, "that girl is Sir Hewitt's daughter."

"Good God," muttered Thornbury, and the others laughed.

* * *

Gillian could not help but be impressed by the ballroom of Lady Bickerstaff. It seemed so enormous and very beautiful with the huge crystal chandeliers ablaze with candlelight. She had never before seen such an assortment of splendidly dressed ladies and gentlemen and she thought the gowns very fine and the men very dashing.

Lady Meg Fairfax took pleasure in Gillian's reaction. It was rare to find anyone who would get excited over anything these days. An air of practiced boredom was generally the rule, and it was refreshing to see how Gillian's eyes grew wide at the sight of the room.

"It is so very grand," whispered Gillian, and Meg smiled.

"You may not think so after a time. There are bound to be some of the worst bores here tonight."

"Bores? I don't think anyone here could be the least bit boring. Oh, who is that?"

Meg followed Gillian's gaze toward a portly middle-aged man surrounded by other guests. "Oh, that is Mr. Phillips."

"Oh," said Gillian. "He looked very important and I thought perhaps he was the prince."

"Oh, good heavens, no," said Meg, bursting into laughter. "Prinny is far grander than that, and as I have said, he shall grace us with his presence later in the evening. Come, I see some friends I should like you to meet."

Gillian nodded and the two ladies made their way through the crowd.

Lady Honoria Ashley cast a critical gaze upon the company assembled in the Bickerstaff home. She was not well-acquainted with most of the ladies and gentlemen in attendance, an unfortunate circumstance attributed to her husband's refusal to become involved in London society.

Lord Ashley never came to town and spent all his time at his estate at Woodbridge. It was not until Lady Ashley's daughter, Christobel, had married that Lady Ashley had a very good excuse to come to town. Christobel loved to be in the thick of things and spent much of her time in London.

Lady Ashley regarded her daughter with motherly affection and pride. She had done very well for herself, it seemed. Christobel had married a very wealthy man, and if Freddy Stourbridge was a rather silly, witless fellow, what did it signify? He was very well connected and he enjoyed society as much as Christobel did.

Unfortunately, Lady Ashely's husband did not view Freddy Stourbridge in the same light as she did. His lordship detested his daughter's husband, and a frightful row had ensued when Christobel announced her intention to marry with or without her father's blessing. Seventeen-year-old Christobel had had her way and now a year had passed. Lord Ashley still detested Freddy Stourbridge, but Lady Ashley was certain he would come around very soon.

"What are you thinking about, Mama?"

"Oh, nothing."

"Really, you looked very deep in thought. Hardly the thing for this party. Of course, it is a rather dull gathering."

Freddy Stourbridge, who was standing beside his wife, nodded. "Indeed so, my dear. I say, isn't that Tommy Weatherfield over there? Come let us say hello."

"Oh, darling," exclaimed Christobel, "you cannot be serious. You know I cannot abide Tommy Weatherfield. But you go on, dearest. I know you are dying to talk to him about some silly horse or other."

Freddy grinned, thankful that he had such an understanding wife. "Very well, but I'll be back soon."

Lady Ashley watched him walk away. "He is a good-hearted man, isn't he?"

"My dear Mama, he is nothing if not that. I am always saying that he is too good-hearted. Why, the servants take advantage. They do not take advantage of me."

"Why, isn't that Lady Cavendish? Oh, dear, she is coming this way."

Lady Ashley was not at all happy to see a much-disliked acquaintance coming her way. However, there was nothing she could do but hide her annoyance as Lady Cavendish greeted them. "How well you both look, Lady Ashley and Mrs. Stourbridge."

Lady Ashley acknowledged the compliment with a nod and Christobel looked indifferent. "I hope you are well, Lady Cavendish."

"Oh, very well. But I was rather worried about you. I hope you are not too upset by this rather embarrassing development, shall we say?"

"I'm sure I do not have any idea what you are talking about."

"Then you haven't heard? Oh, my poor Lady Ashley, I do not like to be the one to inform you, but I daresay you should know about it."

"I suggest you tell me, then."

"Oh, certainly. It is that Meg Fairfax has arrived with a certain young lady." Lady Cavendish paused for effect. "The young lady's name is Miss Ashley, Miss Gillian Ashley. She is the daughter of the late Caroline Ashley and Sir Hewitt Gambol. Oh, I know this will conjure up all sorts of dreadful memories for your husband. It is fortunate he is in the country."

Lady Ashley noted the only barely concealed glee with which Lady Cavendish told the tale and tried to suppress her reaction. "How kind of you to inform me of this."

"If you are interested in seeing the young person, you have simply to look for Lady Fairfax. There were so many people around them. Quite a crush of curious individuals. Well, I must be off. It was so nice to see you."

Christobel allowed Lady Cavendish to get out of earshot and then looked incredulously at her mother. "What is she talking about? Does she mean Father's first wife had a child?"

Lady Ashley nodded. "I fear so, but it is the first I have heard of it."

"How dare this person come here calling herself Miss Ashley? She is nothing but a bastard."

"Christobel!"

"That is true, isn't it? How dare she call herself by that name! I am astounded she had the audacity to appear in society."

"I cannot believe it myself. Come, I think we had best have a look at this so-called Miss Ashley."

The mother and daughter made their way across the room, searching for the familiar face of Meg Fairfax. Lady Ashley was acquainted with Lady Fairfax and did not like her. It did not take them look to espy Meg's blond hair and rose-colored gown, and they looked about for the "so-called" Miss Ashley.

"Oh, my God!" Lady Ashley turned suddenly pale and Christobel feared for a moment that she was about to faint.

"What is it?"

"That girl!" Christobel followed her mother's stricken glance until it rested on a very pretty dark-haired girl who was surrounded by half a dozen gentlemen.

Christobel studied the young lady's face, detecting at once something familiar about it. A spark of recognition came to Christobel. The girl bore an unmistakable and almost uncanny resemblance to the portrait of her late Aunt Kathryn that hung in the entrance hallway at her father's estate.

She had grown up with that picture and had often heard her father speak of his only sister. She had died of scarlet fever only three days short of her sixteenth birthday. The laughing girl standing there in the ballroom looked like the tragic Kathryn's twin.

"Christobel, I must go and sit down." Christobel took her mother's arm and the two of them found a quiet corner in which to rest. "Mama, what does it mean? She is so like the portrait and like Father, too. What does it mean?"

"I don't know, Christobel." Lady Ashley frowned. "They are so alike. Thank God your father is not here to see her."

"You don't think she is really Father's child?"

Lady Ashley frowned again. "It is written on her face. Your father would see it in a minute." Lady Ashley reached out and took her daughter's hand and clasped it tightly. "He must never see the girl."

"I doubt he will have the opportunity. But is there no one else who will note the resemblance?"

"Your aunt died before she came out into society and there are few who really knew her. I do not think anyone will discover the likeness. But it will not do to have the girl showing up in drawing rooms all over town calling herself Miss Ashley."

"What can we do?"

"I am not without influence, Christobel, and neither are you. We shall do all we can to make the girl's Season in town a very short one."

"But what can we do?"

"We shall think of something, Christobel. We must." Mother and daughter stared resolutely at each other.

The Earl of Bain nodded to some of his acquaintances as he walked across the ballroom. He had espied his cousin Meg and found himself looking for Gillian Ashley. Since they had parted three days before, he had thought of little else but the angry words they had exchanged. She was a most infuriating young woman, the earl told himself, but he wondered where she was.

His lordship did not have to wonder very long, for his eye soon fell upon Gillian. There she was looking radiantly beautiful in her new blue gown, surrounded by gentlemen. The sight of Gillian smiling and obviously have a wonderful time did not please him. He had not been prepared to see her surrounded by admiring males.

"Oliver."

"Meg." Bain looked down at his cousin, who had come up to take his arm.

"Have you seen Gillian? She looks marvelous and is a great success."

"I am not particularly interested in the young lady."

"Oh, Oliver, the two of you must make up that silly quarrel. Gillian told me all about your Mrs. Rumstead. Really, it is too funny."

"There is nothing funny about it. Your Gillian has no sense of propriety."

"What an old stick you have become, Oliver. But I will not have you quarreling with Gillian. I have grown too fond of her. Look, there is young Renville talking to her. I shouldn't be surprised if she finds herself a duchess one day."

Bain watched Gillian laughing at the young gentleman's remarks and frowned. "I would not be so sure of that, Meg. Renville's parents, the Duke and Duchess of Welbourne, happened to see us the other day. They could not help but recognize Gillian and they will wonder at her traveling about with Mrs. Rumstead, who looked like a charwoman."

"Charwoman? Really, Oliver. I should think they'd wonder more about her traveling about with you. I am glad Mrs. Rumstead was there to chaperone. In the future I hope you will not be so rash as to take Gillian out unattended."

"My dear Meg, I have no intention of going anywhere

with her again. She would probably have me sitting down with street cleaners and chimney sweeps."

"I wish you would stop being absurd. But let us change the subject."

"That is a good idea, Meg. Where is Fairfax? I should like to see that husband of yours again."

"I should like to see him myself, for he is not returned from the country yet. He has promised to be here next week, but he is making me lose all patience. He is always finding excuses for staying out of town. I would think he was avoiding me if I did not know him better."

Bain laughed. "Avoiding you? He adores you."

"That may be, but I should prefer he adore me from a closer distance. Of course, I know how much he detests the London Season. Still, I am tired of hearing his excuses. But is there no sign of Prinny? It is growing late."

"I'm sure he'll turn up soon."

"He had better. I know Gillian will be so disappointed if she does not get to see him."

"I thought we were not going to speak of her."

Meg ignored this remark and waved at Gillian. "Ah, she does see us, Oliver. Come, we must say hello to her."

"No, I think not. I would not want to interrupt her court."

"Oliver, I warn you. I will not tolerate these silly quarrels. What luck. Gillian is coming to us."

Bain watched Gillian approach, and frowned. Why was she so damned beautiful? he wondered.

Gillian regarded Bain curiously. "Good evening, Lord Bain," she said.

"Good evening," he said in a tone that was barely civil.

Gillian resented this reply to her conciliatory manner, and she turned her attention to Meg. "Do you think the Prince Regent will come soon? Lord Renville said he may not come at all."

"Oh, I do hope so, Gillian," replied Meg. "But whether he comes or not, it seems you are having a very exciting night. What do you think of the young gentlemen?"

"They have been very kind."

"And Renville is a nice young man, isn't he?"

"Really, Meg, I have just met him. I admit I am having a nice time, but it is rather exhausting. Everyone is trying so very hard to be charming and witty, and I am trying to be so very charming and witty. Indeed, it is very hard work being charming for any length of time."

Meg laughed. "How true, but you wouldn't know about that, would you, Oliver?" Meg smiled knowingly at Gillian. "Lord Bain is never charming. A gentleman of such consequence does not need to be charming."

The earl gave his cousin a warning look, which she cheerfully ignored.

"Oh, look, there is an old acquaintance of my husband's. Do excuse me."

Bain thought his cousin Meg quite devious in thus abandoning them.

"Lord Bain, do not look so distraught over having to talk to me."

"I didn't think we were on speaking terms, Miss Ashley."

"No, I suppose we are not. But then, that makes it rather awkward." Gillian looked up at Bain's unsmiling countenance, and her lovely face took on a mischievous expression. "If only Mrs. Rumstead were here to fill in the awkward silence."

Bain looked at her for a moment and then burst into laughter.

Gillian smiled. "Truce?"

"Oh, very well."

"Thank goodness. I am sure you are a formidable enemy, my lord. And if I were guilty of being an over-zealous Good Samaritan, I remind you that I was only

following your example. After all, it is you who came to
my aid when I first came to London."

"I wish you wouldn't keep reminding me of that."

"Because you regret it, my lord?"

Bain laughed again. "I must admit I did for a time, but
perhaps I was a trifle intolerant."

"I shall not comment, sir. I wish us to continue speaking
to each other."

Before Bain could reply there was excited murmuring
among the guests.

"What is the commotion?" said Gillian, looking about
the room. The crowd grew suddenly very noisy and then
everyone grew silent.

"The Prince Regent," said Bain.

Gillian's eyes grew wide as she looked toward the door.
A tall portly gentleman had entered the ballroom, and as
he passed, the gentlemen were bowing gravely and the
ladies curtsying very low. Gillian, although very far away
from the Prince Regent, did not miss this opportunity to
drop a much-practiced curtsy. Bain inclined his head
slightly.

"Oh, it must be very exciting to meet him."

The earl, who had spent many an hour in His Royal
Highness's presence, did not share Gillian's excitement.

"He looks rather stern. Is he a difficult man?"

"Difficult is a most apt word for him. He can be very
charming when the mood strikes him, but our prince is a
man of many moods."

"And is that Lady Hertford?"

Bain nodded. "So you know about our prince's lady?"

"Meg told me about her. She looks very amiable. Come,
my lord, let us walk back over there. I wish to get a better
look at His Royal Highness and her ladyship."

"As you command, Miss Ashley," said his lordship, extending his arm.

Gillian laughed and took the proffered arm, and the two of them started back across the ballroom.

Lady Ashley was a woman of strong character, and it did not take her long to recover from the shock of seeing Gillian. She mulled over various courses of action in her mind and concluded that a campaign of well-placed slander might do wonders for ruining the young lady's chances in society.

Her ladyship therefore headed for one of the pillars of society, the formidable Duchess of Welbourne. Fortunately for Lady Ashley, she and the duchess were distantly related, and this tenuous connection had enabled her to make the duchess's acquaintance a number of times.

"Your grace," said Lady Ashley, addressing the duchess.

"Lady Ashley." The duchess's reply was somewhat cold, for she tended to view Lady Ashley with her legion of other social-climbing relations. The duchess was standing with several ladies and gentlemen who were among the assorted hangers-on that followed the duchess.

"I wish to inform your grace of a matter that has just come to my attention. There is a certain young lady here tonight who calls herself Miss Ashley."

One of the hangers-on uttered a disappointed sigh, for she had just been going to inform the duchess of the presence of Gillian.

"Indeed?" The duchess did not seem very interested, but Lady Ashley persisted.

"You may recall that my husband was married before."

"I certainly do. To Caroline Guildford. Such a dreadful scandal that was."

"Caroline had a daughter, and she is here tonight. She goes by the name of Gillian Ashley, although she had no right to the name."

"My poor Lady Ashley, how very dreadful for you."

"Indeed, your grace. You may understand how I feel hearing this creature using my husband's name and mixing with our sort of people."

The duchess nodded. "It is a pity, but one must admire her audacity. Let me think. Who would her father have been?"

One of the other ladies who had been listening intently to this spoke up. "Sir Hewitt Gambol."

This intelligence brought gales of laughter from the duchess and her friends. "Indeed! How very droll! Where is this young lady?"

"There in the blue dress," said Lady Ashley.

"I see her, your grace," said one of the hangers-on helpfully. "She is standing with the Earl of Bain."

The Duchess of Welbourne took up her quizzing glass and pointed it in Gillian's direction. "Oh, yes, I see her. Why, I do believe she is the one I saw with Bain the other day."

Lady Ashley quickly took a cue from this remark. "Your grace is well aware of Lord Bain's reputation. She is hardly a credit to the Ashley name."

"She was not alone with him," said the duchess. "There was also a dreadful-looking woman and a little boy. The woman was very stout and badly dressed. She was quite vulgar-looking. For a moment I took her for the Princess of Wales." All the hangers-on laughed at this insult to the scandalous wife of the Prince Regent.

"She was doubtless some relation to this Gillian, your grace. The girl is really very common."

"Oh, I don't know about that," said one of the hangers-on. "I thought her quite charming. And Lord Renville told me that she was by far the most interesting young lady in town this Season."

"Did he, indeed?" The duchess looked coldly at the lady who had said these words. Although her grace might think it amusing that Sir Hewitt Gambol's natural daughter appear at fashionable gatherings, she did not think it at all funny that her son and heir find her so attractive. It would not do for the future Duke of Welbourne to become interested in an ill-begotten nobody.

"We shall see about this matter, Lady Ashley," said the duchess, and Lady Ashley smiled triumphantly.

At first Gillian thought she was imagining it, but as the time passed, it became apparent that the attitude of those at the ball had changed toward her and the change was not for the better. When she and Bain had rejoined Lady Meg Fairfax, Gillian thought she detected a few of the ladies regarding her with hostility.

The young gentlemen who had earlier been vying for her attention had seemed to melt away, and although those she had promised dances did come to claim them when the music started, they seemed suddenly cold and distant.

"What is going on?" Meg Fairfax took Bain's arm. "Good heavens, Gillian is being snubbed."

"What are you talking about? You said yourself she is a great success."

"Something has happened. Why, all the young gentlemen are avoiding her, and look at how that dreadful Duchess of Welbourne is scowling at her."

Bain looked across the ballroom floor and saw the duchess staring grimly at Gillian, who was at that moment dancing with a very tall young gentleman with red hair.

"Why, it appears the Duchess of Welbourne is behind this. You said she saw you and Gillian with that Rumstead woman. Yes, of course, she is worried her son Renville is becoming infatuated with Gillian. Well, I will not have Gillian treated this way. She is such a sweet girl. I am going to get to the bottom of this."

Bain started to tell his cousin to forget the Duchess of Welbourne, but Meg Fairfax headed off in the direction of the duchess before Bain could stop her. Bain knew his cousin was at times impulsive, and in order to keep her from doing anything she might regret, he followed after her.

The duchess did not appear very happy to see Meg Fairfax and Bain. She had never liked Meg, and although she was a close friend of Bain's mother, she disapproved heartily of the earl.

"Duchess," said Meg, smiling graciously.

"Ah, Lady Fairfax and Lord Bain." The duchess spoke civilly and the assorted hangers-on flocked around to hear the conversation. Her grace made a few innocuous remarks about the weather and then, not wanting to disappoint her followers, remarked, "I see you have taken a young lady under your wing."

"Yes, your grace. Gillian Ashley, a very charming young lady."

"Oh, yes, I have heard all about her." The duchess looked over at Bain. "It seems you have made her acquaintance, Lord Bain."

Bain did not like the duchess and found himself growing irritated at her insinuation. The Duchess of Welbourne turned to one of her court. "Lord Bain and Miss Ashley were squiring the most extraordinary lady around some days ago. I believe there was a little boy with you, too. Relations of Miss Ashley, I presume."

"They were no such thing," Bain said hotly.

"Bain!" Meg put a restraining hand on her cousin's arm. She looked sweetly at the duchess. "I am surprised you did not guess the identity of the lady and her son."

"Meg, what are you—"

Lady Fairfax cut off her cousin. "Oh, I know it is a secret and I shan't say anything more."

Bain regarded Meg in bewilderment and the duchess looked puzzled. "Who were they?" she said. "I demand you tell me."

"I am afraid, ma'am, that when certain rather eccentric

personages travel incognito, one is honor-bound not to reveal their true identities."

The Duchess of Welbourne thought back to her glimpse of the common-looking woman in Bain's carriage. Had there been a slight resemblance to the Prince Regent in that heavy face? "Not one of the Hanoverian relations?" said her grace, alluding to the Prince Regent's German connections.

"Your grace!" Meg looked at her in mock horror. "You are a very discerning woman, ma'am, but I have said nothing. I hope you will keep such suspicions to yourself."

The Earl of Bain was having a difficult time keeping from bursting into laughter. His cousin had convinced the Duchess of Welbourne that Mrs. Rumstead and little Alfred were the prince's royal cousins. The duchess looked triumphant.

Meg looked contritely at Bain. "Oh, I am sorry, Oliver."

"Meg," he said, somehow managing to keep a straight face, "I want a word with you. Excuse us, Duchess."

Bain led his cousin across the room and out the doors into the garden, where he laughed harder than he had in years.

"What is happening, you two?" Gillian had not expected to find Meg and Lord Bain laughing together. She had seen them go into the garden just as her dance was ending, and eager to join them, had followed them there.

"Oh, Gillian, it is too funny."

"What is it, Meg?" Gillian found herself starting to laugh even though she had not heard the joke.

"My cousin," Bain managed to say at last, "has just made the Duchess of Welbourne believe that the woman she saw in the carriage with us—" Bain laughed again. "That your Mrs. Rumstead was a Hanoverian princess."

"Mrs. Rumstead?" Gillian looked questioningly at Meg, who nodded. Gillian joined them in their laughter and it was some time before the three of them were able to join the party once more.

His Royal Highness, the Prince Regent, was growing dangerously bored. He had not really wanted to come to this ball, for he had been somewhat put out with the evening's host, Sir Gerald Bickerstaff. Sir Gerald had made a remark about the prince's newest race horse that was not at all complimentary, and the remark had come back to the royal ears embellished a little for even greater effect.

Persuaded by Lady Hertford to attend, the Prince Regent was rather cold to the Bickerstaffs and in general rather disagreeable. The charm and affability for which he was famous was conspicuously lacking.

"I daresay, madam, this party is exceeding dull."

"It is very dull, sir." Lady Hertford nodded in agreement.

"What are they whispering about over there?"

"Whispering, sir?"

"Dash it, I've been watching Lady Cavendish over there and she's been rushing about with some tale. I wish to hear it."

"Shall I fetch her, Your Royal Highness?" One of the prince's aides spoke up.

"No, I will not waste my time with her. But find out what she has been spreading about. I don't like gossip I have not heard."

The aide hurried off to do the prince's bidding and returned shortly.

"Well, sir?"

"It seems there is a certain young lady present here tonight, a Miss Ashley. She is the daughter of Caroline Ashley, the former Caroline Guildford. Your Royal Highness may remember the case. The divorce received much publicity."

"Ashley? Oh, yes. I do recall the matter."

"The girl is here under the patronage of Lady Fairfax. It is being said that she is really the daughter of Sir Hewitt Gambol."

"Gambol. My word, that is interesting."

"The Duchess of Welbourne has been encouraging everyone to snub this Miss Ashley."

"The Duchess of Welbourne? Such an awful woman."

Lady Hertford agreed wholeheartedly with the prince's opinion of the duchess. Her ladyship despised the other lady, who had never made any attempt to hide her aversion to Lady Hertford.

"How dreadful that the duchess should seek to speak against the poor girl. I'm sure she is a very nice young lady and does not deserve to be slandered by such as her grace of Welbourne."

Since His Royal Highness was himself the subject of much slander and he had no cause to love the Duchess of Welbourne, he was not at all happy. "I think her grace wields too much power as it is, don't you think, my dear Lady Hertford?"

Lady Hertford nodded. "I fear the girl is ruined in society now that the Duchess of Welbourne has said she disapproves of her."

The remark had the intended effect. "Indeed not, madam. I am the final arbiter of these matters, and the Duchess of Welbourne should learn this. You and I, madam, will see this young lady and lend countenance to her situation."

"You are so very kind, sir."

The prince smiled benignly at his mistress. His spirits were beginning to improve now that he was to play the benevolent monarch. He and Lady Hertford walked across the ballroom, and the crowd parted to allow them to pass. The ladies and gentlemen bowed respectfully and wondered what their prince was up to. They watched with keen interest as he walked directly up to Lady Meg Fairfax, who was standing with the Earl of Bain and a very pretty yound lady dressed in blue.

Meg saw the prince's approach but did not think until he was upon them that he was intending to speak to them. Meg dropped a curtsy and Gillian followed suit. Bain regarded his prince curiously and bowed with more than usual civility.

"Ah, Lady Fairfax. Lady Hertford was just saying how lovely you looked tonight and I wanted to see for myself."

Lady Hertford smiled graciously, and Meg tried to hide her bewilderment. She and Lady Hertford had never been introduced.

"Good evening to you, Bain."

"Good evening, sir."

"And who is this young lady?"

"May I present Miss Gillian Ashley, Your Royal Highness?"

"Charmed. New to town, young lady?"

Gillian met the prince's gaze. "Yes, I have only recently arrived from Edinburgh, Your Royal Highness."

"Edinburgh? And how do you find London?"

"I find it very nice, sir."

"And what do you like best about it?"

"I like Westminster Abbey very much, sir."

"Westminster Abbey?" This comment seemed to amuse the prince. "So that is the highlight of your visit to London?"

"No, sir, the highlight is meeting Your Royal Highness." Gillian spoke with an ingenuous matter-of-factness that delighted the prince.

"Well, I hope we shall be seeing more of you, young lady."

Gillian curtsied again, and the prince and Lady Hertford went on.

"By God, you are a born courtier," said Bain.

"I never thought he would speak to me. He was a very considerate gentleman. And Lady Hertford was most gracious."

"You did very well, Gillian. Prinny was charmed." Meg looked very proud of her charge.

"I hope I didn't sound terribly foolish."

"You were perfect, Gillian," said Bain. "It was just the right amount of awe due our gracious prince."

"You are making fun of me, my lord."

Bain laughed. "I am not. No, indeed, ma'am, I salute you." Bain grinned, thinking that between the prince's attention and the mysterious Hanoverian princess, Gillian Ashley would not be snubbed for long.

Gillian laughed at Bain's expression and was about to say something more when they were suddenly deluged by other guests who wished to speak to Gillian. It seemed, the earl cynically noted, that Miss Ashley was now totally acceptable.

nine

C hristobel Stourbridge returned from a series of afternoon calls and found her mother sitting in the small parlor that they seldom used. "What is this, Mother? Why are you sitting here? It is the dreariest room. I have been telling Freddy that we must redo it. Come, Mama, you would feel much cheerier in the other room."

"I do not feel cheery, Christobel. I have no reason to be happy. Indeed, I do not see how you can go about your business as if nothing is wrong."

"But, Mother, there is little we can do about this Gillian person. The prince has made it quite clear she is to be accepted. All we can do is hope that Father never hears of her, and I daresay I do not see how he can learn of her. He will never leave Ashley Manor and you know that almost no one from town ever visits there."

"Almost no one. That is the problem. There is always the possibility, and who knows what may happen in years to come. I don't know, Christobel. I am very worried about this."

"But, Mama, even if Father did learn of the girl's existence, are you sure it would matter? You don't think he will give her some of my inheritance. I have been his only child for all these years."

"Yes, and if you have forgotten, might I remind you

that he has never accepted Freddy. When you eloped, Ashley threatened to disinherit you. We cannot depend on his paternal feelings for you.''

''But I shall make up with him. You will see. But do not worry, Mama, I have no intention of this Gillian Ashley ever threatening my inheritance. If this were another century, I should consider poisoning her.''

''Christobel!''

''I am only quizzing you, Mama. There must be something that can be done. It certainly did not work trying to ruin her in society. Since Prinny took her up, there was no one willing to snub her. And Meg Fairfax has too many friends.''

''I wonder what the connection between Meg Fairfax and this girl could be. It is very odd how she has taken her under her wing.''

''If only Meg Fairfax would grow to hate her. Perhaps the creature will attempt to steal her husband.''

''Fairfax? From what I've heard he never even looks at another woman, and besides, he is as bad as Ashley. He hardly ever ventures into town.''

''We need to learn more about this girl and about the Fairfax household, Christobel.''

''But how could we do that?''

Lady Ashley looked thoughtful. ''Where there are servants, there are opportunities to find out things. If we had one of Meg Fairfax's servants watching them for us, we might learn something that would help.''

''Why, that is a very good idea, Mama. If we could discover someone willing to share the secrets of the Fairfax household, we may learn something to discredit this Gillian.''

''But we must be very discreet.''

''You need not worry about that, Mama. I assure you all will be done very very discreetly.''

Lady Ashley smiled.

* * *

Lord Bain strode up the walk to Meg Fairfax's door, and as he was about to reach the steps, a young man exited the front door. The young man tipped his hat respectfully to the earl and walked on. Bain watched him for a moment and wondered what Gillian thought of the fellow. He was obviously one of her suitors.

Bain was admitted by the butler and quickly ushererd into the ladies' presence.

"Oliver, how good of you to call." Meg greeted her cousin with a sisterly kiss on the cheek.

"Good day, Lord Bain." Gillian smiled and Bain experienced an unusual sensation he did not really wish to acknowledge. He feared he was growing dangerously fond of the girl and knew he should watch himself. He was more than ten years her senior and had no desire to make a fool of himself.

"It seems I am not your only caller."

"Indeed not, Oliver. Gillian has had four gentlemen callers today and I would not doubt if some are considering making her an offer."

"Meg! Really, Lord Bain, Meg is being quite ridiculous. I wish you would not embarrass me so."

Meg smiled. "I am trying to determine which of the suitors would be the best, but Gillian will not assist me in the least. She refuses to tell me which of them she likes best. There are some very admirable prospects, however."

"Please, Meg! Really, I think it would be better if I persuaded my father to give me a tiny cottage on some island, perhaps in the Hebrides, and I could retire there to peace and quiet."

"My dearest Gillian, you could not be so cruel to all the young men about town."

Gillian turned to Bain. "You see what I must put up with? She is terrible."

The butler interrupted the conversation by appearing at the doorway. "What is it, Hull?"

"A package has just been delivered for miss, my lady."

"For me?" Gillian looked surprised.

"Do give it to her, then, Hull," said her ladyship. "We are all dying of suspense."

The butler bowed and handed a small paper-covered parcel to Gillian. "I cannot imagine who would be sending me gifts."

"One of your many admirers, no doubt," said Meg with a smile. "The card is probably inside."

Gillian tore off the paper to reveal a handsome little case, and she opened it up and gasped. "Oh, dear! Meg, look!"

Gillian handed Meg the case and Lady Fairfax took it eagerly. "Good heavens, Oliver. Emeralds!"

The earl looked at the contents of the box. There sitting upon the velvet was a necklace of emeralds. The stones were of a rare beauty, unmatched by anything Bain had ever seen.

There was a tiny slip of paper inside and Gillian unfolded it. " 'To my dear daughter from her Papa, Sir Hewitt Gambol.' My goodness, they must be worth a fortune."

"Indeed they must. Your papa has a very good eye for stones." Lord Bain studied the necklace. In earlier days he had bought a good deal of jewelry for his various mistresses, but generous as he had been in his extravagant youth, he had never purchased a necklace of that quality.

"I cannot allow him to do this," Gillian said.

"But he obviously wished you to have them," said Meg.

"But it is far too much. Why, it is so expensive as to be positively sinful. I am going to visit him right now and tell him so."

"Now, Gillian, I do not think that it is a good idea for

you to visit him. You must both realize that your association is not for the best."

"But I must go. Will you come, too, Meg?"

"My dear, I do not wish to visit Sir Hewitt, and besides, I am expecting a call from Mrs. Blakely. I cannot be absent and I suggest you stay too."

Gillian turned her blue eyes upon Bain. "Will you go with me, my lord?"

Bain looked questioningly at Meg, who said, "Oh, very well, Oliver, if you are willing to take her, I shan't object, but I do not like it and I hope you will hurry back."

Gillian promised she would do so and soon she and Bain were in the earl's carriage heading for Sir Hewitt's house. Gillian opened up the case that held the emeralds and studied the necklace again. "What could have possessed him to do such a strange thing?"

"Strange? You are his daughter and he is obviously happy to have a child after all these years."

"But I have met him only once." Gillian closed the case. "And he should not be wasting his money on me."

Bain looked over at Gillian and realized that he had finally met a female who seemed to resent expensive presents. He found it a most unusual attitude.

Sir Hewitt's servant admitted them into the baronet's presence. They found Sir Hewitt sitting in a chair, his foot bound with bandages and propped up on a footstool.

"What's this? Company?" The elderly man was obviously delighted to see Gillian.

"Hello, Papa. What is wrong with your foot? You have not been hurt?"

"You see that, sir?" cried Sir Hewitt, addressing Bain. "The lass cares about her poor papa. What a kind-hearted girl. Don't worry, my girl. 'Tis only the gout flaring up. But what are you doing calling on me? Don't forget what Lady Fairfax said. You should not be here."

"Nonsense. I will not give up seeing my own father."

Sir Hewitt grinned. "You're a Gambol, true enough."

"But are you in pain, Papa?"

Sir Hewitt tried to be stoical. "Not so bad, my dear. Come and sit down beside me." He looked up at Bain. "It is young Mr. Bain, is it not?"

"It is the Earl of Bain, Papa. He is Lady Fairfax's cousin."

"Earl? Of course. You succeeded your brother. I do remember now. I barely recognized you, sir. I remember that pair of bays you had. God, they were the damnedest bit of blood and bone. I won one hundred guineas on you once, sir. The time you raced young Harrowby to Brighton. There's not a man who can touch you at the ribbons, sir. You haven't still got those horses?"

"No, I do not." Bain's expression had grown suddenly morose, and Gillian hurried to change the subject. She knew very well that the earl did not want to be reminded of his fame as a whip.

"I received this gift, Papa." Gillian held out the case containing the emeralds. "Really, Papa, it was a lovely thing for you to do, but truly I cannot accept them."

Sir Hewitt looked surprised and a little hurt. "What do you mean? Didn't you like them?"

"Of course I liked them. But, dear Papa, they are not unlike the crown jewels. They must have cost a fortune. I wish you would take them back. They are far too grand for me."

"There's nothing too grand for my daughter. I'll take nothing back."

"But have you forgotten that we have just met?"

"Nay, I've not forgotten, but good God, girl, I've nearly twenty years to make up to you. I'll not hear another word. Tell her, Bain, that she'd best be sensible and take them."

"I think you had," said the earl, rather amused.

"Oh, very well, but I will be furious if you waste any more on me. Meg has said you have sent her a very generous allowance for me. Thank you so much, Papa."

"I hope Lady Fairfax is taking you out into the town."

"Indeed she is, Papa." Gillian grinned. "I have spoken to the prince himself."

"What? That damned bounder!"

"Papa!" Gillian was horrified.

"A plague on him and all his Hanoverian ancestors. Usurpers they are! 'Tis a Stuart who should sit upon the throne."

The Earl of Bain had some difficulty in keeping his composure. He had known that Sir Hewitt Gambol was an eccentric personage, but he had no idea that he harbored these treasonous Jacobite sympathies.

Gillian was clearly thunderstruck.

"It is fortunate, Sir Hewitt," Bain said, "that the prince does not realize your feelings. I doubt if he would have been so courteous to your daughter. His attention has assured her acceptance by all in society. Usurper or no, royal George is Prince Regent of the kingdom."

Sir Hewitt considered this. "Perhaps I was somewhat hasty. He was courteous to you, Gillian?"

"Very much so. Perfectly charming, and since he showed me such consideration, no one else would dare be rude to me."

"They had better not be rude to you. I'll not suffer any offense given to my daughter."

"I assure you, I have been treated extremely well by everyone. I could never have dreamed of being so well-received. Meg says I am a great success, but I think she exaggerates."

Sir Hewitt grinned. "You're a charmer and I bet the lads are already calling by the dozens. They'd be fools if they didn't."

"Hardly by the dozens. But I do not want to talk about

myself any longer. I am worried about you. Have you seen the doctor?"

"Doctor? By all that's holy they're naught but charlatans and windbags. I'll not allow them in the door."

"Then who saw to your leg?"

"Moffat."

"Moffat? You mean the butler?"

"He's a capable man."

"Papa, that is quite ridiculous. I will find you a good physician. No, do not argue. I am very serious!"

"Bossy wench, isn't she?" said Sir Hewitt to Bain. "Hear this, my girl, I'll not take orders from you."

"You will indeed, sir. Now, when did you last eat?"

"Eat? What are you talking about?"

"What did you have for luncheon?"

"I don't recall. Oh, yes, a bit of mutton."

"A bit of mutton, and what else?"

"God in heaven, girl. Oh, very well, some brandy and . . . Oh, what does it signify?"

"It is very important. Tell him, Lord Bain."

Although his lordship did not wish to become embroiled in a family argument, Gillian's stern look made him say that sufficient nourishment was doubtlessly important.

"Now, I will find your kitchen and see what can be done."

"You'll do no such thing."

"I am a very good cook and I shall fix you something. No, you can do nothing about it." Gillian got up. "Do stay with Papa, Bain. I shall be back shortly."

Although the earl was not at all happy about the prospect of staying there with Sir Hewitt, he had little choice. He looked across at Sir Hewitt and the elderly man grinned at him. Bain had never been good at small talk, and the two men sat there staring at each other.

"Quite a young lady," said Sir Hewitt, finally breaking the silence.

"Oh, yes, Gillian is a fine girl."

"A trifle bossy. She gets it from the Hewitt side. Her mother was meek as a lamb. She's getting on all right?"

"More than all right. That young lady created quite a sensation at Lady Bickerstaff's ball. The Prince Regent . . ." Bain paused and looked over at Sir Hewitt to see if the mention of the prince would cause him to erupt into another tirade, but Sir Hewitt kept silent. "The Prince Regent was quite charmed with Gillian. If she wishes to be a great society lady, she can very easily accomplish that goal. And I do not doubt that she can have her pick of any number of eligible men."

Sir Hewitt nodded thoughtfully. "A girl has got to get married, but the fellow who weds Gillian had better treat her well or he'll have to answer to Hewitt Gambol."

Bain did not know what to reply to this, and Sir Hewitt did not give him the opportunity to speak. Suddenly talkative, the baronet began to reminisce about the horses he had ridden as a young man, and this subject kept him quite occupied until Gillian returned and announced that she had prepared him some supper. The earl was quite glad when Sir Hewitt's talk was stopped by the advent of the food, and gladder still when he and Gillian said farewell to the eccentric baronet.

ten

The Earl of Bain was depressed. He sat listlessly in his sitting room and glanced from time to time at the pages of a new novel he had just begun to read. The book did not interest his lordship and he had difficulty concentrating on it. Finally he put it down.

He glanced at the mantel clock and frowned. It was nearly eight o'clock and he had promised to take his mother to Almack's. He had not seen her since their last meeting, and how unsatisfactory that meeting had been. He did not doubt that she would still be upset with him, and the thought of accompanying her to Almack's was gloomy indeed.

At the best of times the earl found Almack's exclusive assembly rooms exceedingly dull. In his present mood he could hardly bear the thought of going. It took all of his lordship's self-control to force himself to rise from his chair. He had no choice. He must pick up his mother at her house and proceed to Almack's.

He was in no better mood when he arrived at his mother's house. The dowager countess greeted him coolly. "It is rather late, Oliver. I had begun to think you weren't coming."

"I said I would take you, Mama, and here I am."

"If it is such an onerous duty to accompany me, I should prefer to stay home."

"Please, Mama, let us not quarrel."

"Very well, Oliver. It is late, and if we are going to go, I daresay we should be off."

The earl nodded and the two of them left the house. As he assisted his mother into the carriage, Bain reflected that the evening was not getting off to a very auspicious start.

The dowager countess sat quietly for a time as they made their way toward Almack's. Finally, she broke her silence. "The Duchess of Welbourne called on me yesterday afternoon. She said she saw you riding about town with a Miss Ashley and a woman she suspects was the Grand Duchess of Coburg and her son the crown prince. Why did you not tell me about this?"

To his mother's surprise, Bain burst into laughter.

"What is so funny, Oliver?" demanded her ladyship.

"Really, Mother, how could you believe such bosh? Grand duchess, indeed."

"Then who was this woman?"

"She was . . . an acquaintance of Miss Ashley's. She is not known in town."

"Is it bosh that your cousin Meg has taken this Miss Ashely person into her house and that you are fequently seen with her? The duchess said you and she were often together at Lady Bickerstaff's ball."

"She is a very nice young lady, Mama."

"She is the illegitimate daughter of Sir Hewitt Gambol! I warn you, Oliver, if you have any ideas of marrying this girl, you had best forget them quickly. I will never approve of such a match."

"God in heaven, Mother, I have said nothing about marriage. Why must you make so much of nothing?"

Lady Bain looked closely at his lordship. "I simply want to make myself clear on the matter."

Bain made no reply. He resolved to say little else to his mother, and her ladyship seemed quite happy with this arrangement. The mother and son rode in silence the rest of the way to the assembly rooms.

The dowager countess immediately attached herself to some of her friends and left Bain to prowl about the punch bowl and reflect that his was at that moment a most miserable existence.

"Oliver?"

The earl looked up startled. His friend John Colville stood before him. "John. Thank God, a friendly face. It seems my luck is changing."

"What is wrong, old fellow? You look dashed awful, if you will forgive my bluntness."

Bain took a sip of his punch. "I don't know, John. I am in one of my moods. You know all about that."

Colville, who was well-acquainted with the earl's black moods, smiled. "I take it Lady Bain is about somewhere."

The earl nodded. "I believe she disapproves more and more of me each day. I can do nothing to please her."

"Then perhaps you had best give up trying."

Bain nodded. "Perhaps you are right, John."

Just as he was beginning to be buoyed by his friend's company, they were joined by Henrietta Colville, who was, in Bain's eyes, a most unwelcome intruder. Mrs. Colville smiled at the earl. "Are you men hiding over here? We ladies will not have it."

"Have you broken away from Mrs. Hibbert so soon, my dear?"

"Indeed I did. I could not bear to hear of her abominable little brats any longer. The woman is perfectly obsessed with those children of hers. One should send one's children off to school and think no more about them."

The sight of Henrietta Colville returned the earl to his gloomy state. He wanted nothing to do with her. She looked sweetly at her husband. "John, darling, Lady Rutherford was asking for you and I promised I'd send you over. Don't worry. I'll entertain his lordship here."

"Oh, very well. I'll be back shortly. Henrietta will keep you amused."

Henrietta Colville cast a shrewd glance at the earl. "So here we are again, Bain."

"Yes, so it seems."

"I think John so touchingly naive, don't you? He doesn't suspect a thing between us."

Bain glared at her. "There is nothing between us, madam."

"I'm not so sure of that, Bain. I recollect how you behaved on a certain visit. Oh, I think it so very sweet how you keep up this facade of loyalty to poor John. You were old school chums, after all, and he thinks you are the greatest man next to Wellington. But I know you, my lord. I know what sort of a man you are and I know that you want me as much as I want you."

The earl tried very hard to hold his temper. "I will try to make this clear to you, Mrs. Colville. I will have nothing to do with you, now or ever. I shall be civil to you for John's sake, but if possible, I shall shun you like the very devil."

To his lordship's surprise, Henrietta Colville only laughed and cast him a knowing look.

"Good evening, madam." The earl walked away from Mrs. Colville and started across the room. The orchestra was beginning to play and he impulsively asked the first lady he happened to meet to dance. The young lady, who had been just lamenting the dearth of gentlemen, was quite astonished to find herself in the arms of the wild Earl of Bain. They did not talk as they danced, and afterward the earl led his partner back to her companions.

The young lady's mother, who had never before considered the wealthy earl as a prospective bridegroom, began to consider the matter and latched on to his lordship, asking him numerous questions. Bain somehow replied civilly and was about to extricate himself from the ladies when a short thin gentleman came upon them.

"I say, ladies, sir, did you hear what Lady Ashley was saying?"

"And what was that, Uncle Rupert?" said the earl's former dancing partner. Bain was suddenly interested.

"I do not like to spread gossip, of course, but yesterday Lady Ashley told me about this young Miss Ashley who is being introduced by Lady Fairfax." No one seemed to know his lordship's connection with Lady Fairfax, and the gentleman continued. "She is actually Sir Hewitt Gambol's daughter. Can you imagine? Well, the prince has favored her with a few words and therefore lent respectability to her. However, Lady Ashley has been making inquiries and it seems she has revealed all sorts of dreadful things about the young person's character."

Lord Bain frowned ominously. "What things, sir?"

The gentleman looked over at his niece as if uncertain whether she was old enough to hear his revelation. Since her mother made no attempt to stop him, he continued. "She was abandoned at a very early age to make her own way on the streets of Edinburgh." Uncle Rupert gave his lordship a knowing look. "Shall we say she had a good many 'protectors' before coming to London to try to pass herself off as a respectable lady. How Lady Fairfax has become involved is still unknown."

"You are speaking rot, sir."

"I beg your pardon." Uncle Rupert looked at Bain as if he had not heard him correctly.

"I said you are speaking goddamned rot, sir. How dare you repeat such utter rubbish."

Bain's former dancing partner looked for a moment as if she were about to have an attack of the vapors.

Uncle Rupert grew quite red in the face. "How dare you use that tone of voice with me."

"God damn it, were you not such a repellent little man, I should knock you down. You are no gentleman to cast aspersions upon the character of a lady whom you know nothing about. How dare you spread these lies."

"Lord Bain!" The mother of the young lady about to faint called his name sharply.

Uncle Rupert, who had not realized the identity of this belligerent gentleman, looked at him in surprise. He was well-acquainted with Oliver Bain's reputation and was not so foolhardy as to demand satisfaction from a man reputed to be one of the best shots in the kingdom.

"Lord Bain, I suggest you leave," said the young lady's mother.

"Willingly, madam." The earl stalked off, and then remembering his mother, he sought her out. He found her among her friends and she seemed to be enjoying herself. Her ladyship looked questioningly up at her son, who looked very grim.

"I am going home now. If you wish to go with me, you will come at once."

The dowager countess was stunned. She looked at her friends and noted the startled expressions on their faces. She hesitated for a moment as if debating over her response. "Very well, Oliver. You go ahead. I shall join you as soon as I make my farewells."

Bain walked off and stood awaiting his mother. He waited for some time and grew increasingly irritated. Finally, she joined him and very calmly took his arm.

When they arrived outside, Lady Bain exchanged her calm demeanor for an expression of rage. "How dare you humiliate me in front of everyone. I shall never forgive you for this, Oliver."

Bain remained silent.

"What has come over you? Oh, I heard all about what happened and your conduct tonight was deplorable. How could you have spoken to Rupert Littlefield like that?"

"The man is an ass."

"The room was buzzing with talk. It was told you nearly attacked poor Rupert just because he was saying something about this Gillian Ashley person. Lord knows, Oliver, he is only repeating what everyone else is saying. I know Meg has taken the girl under her wing, but what does she really know about her? If she is Gambol's daughter, she has bad blood, you can be sure of that."

"Hang it, Mother, I will not have you parroting that nonsense."

The dowager countess stared at her son. "Don't tell me this girl is another of your bits of fluff. In God's name, why haven't you ever been able to form an attachment to a respectable girl?"

"Damn it, Mother. Gillian is not my mistress, and I'll not have you slandering her."

Lady Bain regarded her son with a hurt expression. "I have done nothing to deserve this sort of treatment from you, Oliver. You always were a cruel, thoughtless boy."

The earl did not trust himself to reply but stared grimly at his mother across the darkened space of the carriage interior. He said nothing further, and when the carriage stopped at Lady Bain's house, he did not even attempt to show her to the door, but motioned for the footman to do so. He was grateful for the darkness as the carriage pulled away.

eleven

"I really think everything is going splendidly, don't you, Gillian?"

Gillian looked up from her book. "What is going splendidly?"

"You know very well I mean that you are doing extremely well. We have received so many invitations that we cannot attend them all. I think your first Season will be an unqualified success."

Gillian smiled indulgently at Lady Fairfax and put down the book. They were sitting in the drawing room after a quiet and delicious luncheon, and Gillian was enjoying the rest after several days of social engagements that she found as wearying as they were enjoyable.

"If I am a success, I have you to thank, Meg. You have been wonderful to me and—"

Meg cut her off sharply. "I will not listen to another expression of gratitude, so do not attempt it."

"Very well, Meg. I shan't say another thank-you, but I am very grateful."

"Gillian! Well, my girl, I daresay you will not be quite so grateful when I tell you where we are going this afternoon."

"This afternoon? Oh, Meg, I thought we might stay here."

"You forget that it is Thursday, and Thursday is my day to make calls. What would everyone think if I failed to do so?" Meg looked over at the mantel clock. "And I think we should think about getting started. We must call upon Letitia Cavendish, and I so abhor seeing that woman that if I hesitate much longer, I shall lose my resolve."

"You don't mean we must go see Lady Cavendish? Why, I thought you detested her."

"My dear girl, if one limited one's calls to one's friends, one would make very few calls."

Gillian shook her head. "I sometimes think the ways of society are most perplexing, but if we must make some calls, I had best get ready."

"And I too. Let us make haste. We leave within the half-hour."

Gillian nodded somewhat reluctantly and the two ladies left the drawing room to hasten to their rooms.

A short time later they found themselves inside Lady Cavendish's stylishly decorated drawing room, discussing the Prince Regent. They had not been engaged in this discussion for very long when Lady Cavendish's butler entered the room and announced the arrival of two more callers.

Lady Cavendish studied the calling cards the butler had given her and looked very pleased. "I do hope you would not mind seeing two more guests," said Lady Cavendish.

"Indeed not," said Meg quite sincerely, for she did not doubt the conversation would be much improved if not limited to Lady Cavendish's prattle.

"Do show them in," Lady Cavendish commanded the butler, who bowed and left them.

Gillian wondered at the identity of the callers, since their hostess was obviously quite delighted at their arrival. She watched the door and saw two well-dressed ladies enter. Glancing over at Meg, Gillian was surprised at her expression. Meg was obviously acquainted with these newcomers and did not seem at all pleased to see them.

Lady Cavendish noted Meg's expression with satisfaction. The two ladies stopped short at seeing Gillian and Meg. The elder of the newcomers frowned ominously.

"My dear Lady Ashley," said Lady Cavendish, "how good of you to call, and how good to see you, Mrs. Stourbridge."

Gillian regarded the new visitor strangely. So this was Lady Ashley, the woman who had married Lord Rowland Ashley, her mother's husband. And this was Christobel Stourbridge. She studied the two ladies, thinking them both very attractive despite the grim expressions of their faces. The mother and daughter were alike in many ways, and their relationship was obvious.

There was an awkward silence as Lady Ashley stared at Meg. She seemed to be debating whether to turn around and leave. Lady Cavendish noticed this and hastened to fill the void. "I believe you know Lady Fairfax, don't you? But I daresay you have not met Miss Ashley." It seemed abominable to Gillian that Lady Cavendish seemed to be enjoying herself so much. She resolved to keep her feelings to herself and give Lady Cavendish no further satisfaction.

"I have met these ladies," said Meg pleasantly, "although we are not very well-acquainted."

"Do sit down, ladies," said Lady Cavendish, ushering her new guests into the room and into chairs across from Meg and Gillian.

Christobel Stourbridge did not seem at all happy at the prospect of spending time with them. She stared across at Gillian with an expression of undisguised contempt.

"And how is your husband, Lady Ashley?" began Lady Cavendish. "We see so little of him. Why, I daresay he hasn't been to town for many years."

"My husband is very well, thank you," replied Lady Ashley coldly. There was silence as the two sets of ladies studied each other like opposing pugilists.

The silence was broken by the appearance of the butler.

"I am sorry, my lady, but there is a messenger from the Princess of Wales and he won't give this letter to anyone but your ladyship."

Lady Cavendish smiled a self-important smile.

"Oh, how very tedious. I shan't be a moment." She hurried off as if worried that her guests would bolt from her drawing room before she returned, and indeed, the thought had crossed Gillian's mind.

The four ladies sat in silence a few moments longer and then Christobel Stourbridge spoke. "And so we meet," she said, directing this comment to Gillian. "You are the so-called Gillian Ashley."

"Christobel." Lady Ashley gave her daughter a warning look, but Christobel ignored it and continued.

"One must admire your audacity, trying to succeed in society."

"It seems, Mrs. Stourbridge," said Meg, "that Miss Ashley is not 'trying' to succeed. She *is* succeeding."

"For the moment." Christobel smiled maliciously at Gillian. "Do not think for a moment that any person of consequence would take you seriously. The daughter of Hewitt Gambol is a curiosity and may be humored for a time, but I assure you you will not be tolerated for long."

Gillian was doing her best to remain calm. "I have done nothing to you, Mrs. Stourbridge, that you should so dislike me."

Christobel let out a short derisive laugh. "Haven't you? You have stolen my father's name, a name to which I do not think you are entitled. You have brought me and my mother up for ridicule."

"She has done nothing of the sort," Meg snapped.

Lady Ashley turned to Meg. "I don't know what you have to gain in sponsoring this girl, Lady Fairfax. Does it give you joy to revive a scandal that has been dead for twenty years? Are you happy that you have brought the name of Caroline Guildford back to light to cause my family nothing but pain and embarrassment? Caroline Guildford was a wicked unfaithful woman and I should not doubt any daughter of hers will be no better."

"How dare you!" Gillian stood up, quite incensed. "Why, you insufferable woman! You know nothing about my mother. I will not have you slander her."

"And I will not have you going about town pretending to be my father's daughter." Christobel Stourbridge had leapt to her feet, and Meg feared for a moment that the two young ladies would come to blows. "Your very presence in London is an insult. Why don't you go back to Scotland where you and that trollop your mother came from!"

Christobel's words destroyed what little self-control Gillian had left, and suddenly enraged, she issued a resounding slap to Christobel's face.

The blow stunned Christobel and brought Lady Ashley to her feet howling like an outraged lioness. "You ill-bred creature!"

"Ladies! Please!" Meg hurried to restore order. "Gillian! Both of you! Calm yourselves!"

Christobel was rubbing her cheek. "I should have expected such treatment from you. Fortunately I am a lady or I should tear your hair out."

Meg managed to place herself between the two young ladies. "Gillian, I think we had better go."

"I should like nothing better." Gillian glared once more at Christobel and Lady Ashley, and then walked off. Meg rushed after her. They passed Lady Cavendish on their way to the door.

"You cannot be leaving?"

"We can indeed," said Meg. "Good day, Letitia."

Lady Cavendish looked very disappointed as Meg and Gillian continued on to the door and then hurried out. Obviously there had been a great row and it was Lady Cavendish's poor luck to have missed it. Her ladyship shrugged and considered that at least Lady Ashley and her daughter were still in the drawing room. She made haste to return to them before they, too, would take flight. Fortunately for Lady Cavendish, the two ladies were sitting calmly in the drawing room when she returned and seemed quite willing to talk of what had transpired there.

Meg was relieved when the carriage rapidly left the Cavendish home behind them. "That horrible woman."

Gillian nodded. "Mrs. Stourbridge is horrible."

"I was referring to Letitia Cavendish. I do not doubt she contrived to have us come together just so she would have some gossip to report."

"It seems she will have much to report. I know I should not have struck her, but I completely lost my temper. I fear I have some Highland blood."

Meg nodded. "Well, it is not too serious. She was not injured, and I think, considering what she said to you, you cannot be faulted. Of course, one never knows what sort of tales Letitia Cavendish will spread about."

"I should not be surprised if everyone in society shuts their doors to me."

"My dear Gillian, you know so little about society. Why, the more Letitia spread stories about you and the more she embellishes them, the better."

Gillian regarded Meg with a puzzled expression.

Meg laughed. "Nothing is better than to be mentioned in society. Those who do not know you will be dying for the opportunity to meet you. Do not be surprised if you receive scores of invitations."

Gillian shook her head and reflected again that the ways of high society were very peculiar.

twelve

I t seemed that Meg was right. Invitations and callers kept streaming into the Fairfax household and Gillian Ashley spent the next two weeks in continuous activity. She was kept so busy with parties, afternoon calls, and trips to the theater that she soon forgot her unfortunate meeting with Christobel Stourbridge and her mother.

If the other members of society had heard about her altercation with Christobel (and Gillian was certain that they had), they did not seem to hold it against her. Indeed, Gillian was becoming more popular each day.

In addition to the flury of social activities, Gillian managed to visit Sir Hewitt Gambol nearly every day. Gillian badgered the wayward baronet into taking care of himself properly and was satisfied that his condition was improving under her watchful eye.

It was a most enjoyable time for Gillian save for one thing: the absence of Lord Bain. He had seemed to vanish from town and Gillian realized that she sorely missed his company. Meg was as puzzled as her young friend by Bain's disappearance. It was unlike him to go so long without calling at the Fairfax house, and the notes Meg sent him prompted short replies that said his lordship would call very soon. Gillian found herself thinking more and more about the earl, but was careful to keep her thoughts to herself.

His lordship, meanwhile, was purposely avoiding the Fairfax household. The quarrel with his mother over the episode at Almack's had plunged him into a terrible melancholy that was compounded when he appeared at his mother's door two days later ready to make peace with her.

At his mother's doorstep the earl was told that her ladyship was indisposed and would not see him. Incredulous at first, Bain protested, and was told in no uncertain terms by his mother's butler that the dowager countess did not wish to see him. Furious, Bain had shouted an oath and had vowed that he would never again come to her. She would come to him or they would never speak again.

He reacted to this injury by going home and drinking himself into a stupor. The following evening he went out at midnight to one of the seedier gaming spots in town and lost a very large sum of money. In the two weeks that followed he continued in this behavior, drinking and gaming away large sums and then hating himself for it the next day.

Gillian and Meg were totally unaware of his lordship's problems. They had not even heard of his estrangement with his mother, for none of Meg's friends cared to enlighten her about it. After two weeks had passed, Gillian went off alone to see Sir Hewitt. Happy for the opportunity to be by herself, she sat in the open carriage, gazed at the horses she was passing, and thought about her life in London.

She had to admit she was enjoying herself. The gaiety, the dancing, and the trips to the theater were all very pleasant. She glanced down at the fine green satin of her pelisse and thought that she must look very different than when she first had come to town. Gillian smiled as she reflected upon her first night in London and how Lord Bain had come to her rescue.

She thought of Bain and sighed. Of all the men of her acquaintance, he was the one she most cared to see. Why had he not called? It was rather odd. They had heard nothing from him in a fortnight. Perhaps he had grown bored with her.

It was a great deal to ask for a sophisticated gentleman like the earl to spend time with someone like herself. After all, she knew very well he considered her a mere girl. Gillian frowned. Perhaps he had a mistress. Most gentlemen did, and she had heard Meg make a few references to "Bain's lady friends." For some reason, the thought of Bain having a mistress was quite distressing. Yet that was the most logical explanation for his long absence.

"Rutledge!"

"Yes, miss?" The carriage driver glanced back at his charge.

"I should like to call upon the Earl of Bain first. Would you be so kind as to take me to his house?"

"Aye, miss."

Gillian sat back in the upholstered seat and continued to watch the passing scenery.

They arrived at his lordship's house a short time later and the groom jumped down to help her from the carriage. Gillian doubted that it was completely proper for unescorted young ladies to call upon gentlemen, but she was not really sure she cared. Society had so many silly rules that she was growing tired of them.

The earl's butler seemed rather surprised and slightly uncomfortable to see the young lady standing at his master's door.

"I would like to see his lordship, if I may," she said. "I am Miss Ashley."

"If you would wait here a moment, miss." The butler

vanished and returned a short time later. "His lordship is not receiving, miss."

"Is he ill? Or does he have other guests?"

"He does not have other guests, miss."

"Then he is ill? Please, I must see him."

"No, miss."

Gillian studied the butler's face and sensed his discomfort. "There is something wrong here and I will know what it is."

Much to the worthy servant's horror, Gillian pushed right past him and entered the earl's drawing room. The butler hurried to stop her, but she was too quick for him. "Bain!"

Gillian stopped short as she beheld the earl. He looked so different that she was at first unsure if he was the same person. Rather than the impeccably dressed gentleman she had known, she found an unshaven disheveled man sitting in his shirt sleeves with his neckcloth all askew. He was holding a wineglass in his hand, and when he saw her, he shouted, "God damn it, man, I told you I was not in."

"I'm sorry, m'lord," the butler managed to say.

"It is not his fault, Bain. I barged right in. I was worried about you."

The earl took a drink of wine. "And so you see I am fine, Miss Ashley."

"No, I don't see that at all." Gillian approached and sat down beside him. "Whatever has happened?"

"Nothing has happened, my dear Gillian. And I do not recall giving you leave to sit down."

Gillian ignored the remark. "You had not come to see us, and Meg and I wondered why."

"I have been extremely busy, miss. And don't you think you had best leave? Don't you fear for your virtue alone with such a disreputable drunken lecher like the Earl of Bain?" He drained the last of the wine in his glass and then shouted for the butler. "More wine, Parker."

"No, Parker, I think not." Gillian surprised herself by the determined way in which she said these words.

Bain looked at her in surprise. "Do you intend to bully me, miss?"

"I do, my lord. Parker, bring his lordship some coffee."

"Yes, miss."

"Dammit, Parker, you'll do no such thing. You'll escort this lady to the door." However, the butler had already vanished, and Bain shook his head. "I'll not be bullied and I am not drunk."

Gillian looked sorrowfully at the earl.

"And I do not need your pity, madam."

"What has happened to cause this, sir? Truly some cataclysm must have occurred." A thought came to Gillian. "It is a woman, isn't it?"

"Isn't it always a woman when a man is miserable?"

Gillian felt somehow hurt by this revelation. "I should have known. You must have loved her very much. But is there no chance she will come back to you?"

Bain looked slightly puzzled and then laughed. "So you think I am mooning over a mistress who has deserted me?"

"Isn't that what happened?"

"God in heaven, no. Now, don't you think you could better spend your time calling upon someone else? Perhaps one of your suitors like the Marquess of Renville."

"I prefer to talk to you."

The butler entered the room at that point with the coffee and looked nervously at his master. "Thank you, Parker," said Gillian, "put it down here." The butler gave a sigh of relief, looking gratefully at Gillian, and put down the coffee service.

"Do you always take over every man's household you come to visit?"

Gillian smiled. "I seem to have got into the habit after visiting my father."

Gillian poured a cup of coffee and handed it to him. "If you care to talk about it, I shall be glad to listen."

The earl took the cup and a sip of the steaming liquid. "God, I hate coffee. And I must look a sight."

Gillian smiled. "I will admit you do not look quite as handsome as usual, but one becomes accustomed to the change."

"I look as bad as that?" Bain managed a smile. "Look here, Gillian, I am sorry. I don't know what I've been doing these past two weeks." He hesitated, as if wondering whether he should continue. "My mother has always said those who turn to drink to forget their woes are nothing but cowards. I think she is right and she's right to despise me."

"Your mother cannot despise you, surely."

"She can and always has. God in heaven, I have never done anything that pleased her. When I was a boy, she told me that she could not understand how my brother Edgar and I could have the same parentage. Edgar was clever and kind and noble, and I was none of those things. At least that is what my dear mama has always thought."

"Poor Bain." Gillian reached over and took his lordship's hand.

"Who would think that a grown man wants nothing more than his mother's love and approval. But that I can never hope to have. After all, she believes it is I who killed Edgar. It is my fault that my noble brother is dead."

"Bain, that is nonsense. You must know it wasn't your fault. Why must you torture yourself? Yes, Meg has told me all about the accident. It was a great tragedy, but you could not have stopped it."

"I did not have to have those accursed horses. I knew they were dangerous, but I was so damned proud of my skills at the reins. I had to prove that no horses were the match for Oliver Bain. Poor Edgar. He was always so staid and sober, always attending to duty. When he asked to try the horses, I knew he had not the skill to handle them. I should never have allowed him to take them."

"Meg said your brother insisted. You tried to stop him, but he would not be dissuaded. It was not your fault."

"That is not what my mother thinks."

"Then she is wrong. Bain, you must believe it. You are not to blame. You are a good man and never wished to harm your brother. You must put this guilt aside. You must, or it will destroy you."

Bain looked questioningly into Gillian's blue eyes for a time. "I'm sorry. I should not have told you this." He shook his head. "I've never talked about it to anyone. Poor Gillian. Those are very young shoulders to have to bear my troubles."

"I am not so young, Bain. At least I do not feel so very young."

He smiled. "You have born your share of sorrow. I am very callous not to think of it. Your mother is not long gone from you."

Gillian nodded. "I think of her all the time. We were very close, perhaps because we only had each other. I do miss her."

The earl pressed Gillian's hand. "Aren't we two sad ones? Come, why don't we go out? I could do with some air. That is, if you aren't ashamed to be seen with me." He grew suddenly serious. "In fact, perhaps you should not be seen with me."

"Whatever can you mean? My dear Lord Bain, I insist you come with me right now. I am going to visit my father and I know how much you would love to see him again."

Bain smiled.

"But I am quite prepared to wait until you reacquaint yourself with a razor, sir."

The earl ran his hand against his stubble on his chin. "You don't think I look dashing?"

Gillian laughed and was glad to see Bain returned to his old self. "Do hurry, my lord."

Gillian watched his lordship leave the room and heard him shout for his valet. He was a very complicated man and it seemed he had great cause for sorrow. What sort of woman could his mother be to act so cruelly toward him?

Gillian wondered about the dowager countess and then thought of the earl. It seemed that her interest in that gentleman was something more than sisterly affection. Gillian sighed. She knew she was his friend and confidante, but did not think he would ever consider her to be anything more.

Some time later Oliver Bain and Gillian arrived at the home of Sir Hewitt Gambol. Bain had recovered himself admirably, and no one, by looking at his well-groomed appearance, would have ever surmised his earlier state. To Gillian's great relief his mood seemed quite changed, and he talked and joked as if nothing at all was the matter.

"I am sorry I am late, Papa," said Gillian, kissing Sir Hewitt on the cheek.

"It is my fault, Gambol," said the earl. "I am afraid I detained Miss Ashley longer than it was my intention to do so."

"Glad I am to see you, both of you."

"Papa, are you feeling unwell? You look rather pale." Gillian was rather alarmed by the baronet's appearance, for he seemed in obvious discomfort.

"I am fine, daughter. No cause for worry. Why don't the two of you sit down. I'll have my man fetch tea."

Gillian and Bain sat down and the earl glanced about the room. It seemed the baronet had made a number of improvements to the house. Bain wasn't sure what had been done to account for the transformation, but the house was not a most pleasant place. He suspected that Gillian had somehow been responsible for the change.

"Is your leg troubling you, Papa?"

"No, no worse than usual." Gillian noted the difficulty with which Sir Hewitt spoke. She was certain his leg was very painful.

"I am not sure you should be up, sir. Perhaps you should be in bed. What did the doctor say?"

"Doctors? Bah! I don't care what the leech said."

"But I do. He was supposed to see you this morning. Did he come?"

"Yes, the fool was here. The damned charlatan!"

"What did he say?"

"He said nothing."

"Oh, you are exasperating, Papa. Where is Moffat? Moffat, come here!"

Sir Hewitt's servant appeared. "Yes, miss?"

"Your master refuses to tell me what the physician said to him this morning. I hope you will tell me."

"He said the master ought to be in bed for several days."

"Traitor!" shouted Sir Hewitt. "Ingrate!"

The servant cowered at this abuse and Gillian tried to soothe him. "Don't worry, Moffat, you have done right in telling me. We shall see Sir Hewitt gets to bed this very instant."

"I'm not an invalid!"

"You will do as the doctor tells you. Lord Bain, will you help me get my father to bed?"

"It is useless to argue with her, Gambol. Your daughter is a very determined young lady. One cannot hope to win against her."

"You're right, Bain. She's got the Hewitt blood, that's very clear. Very well, minx. I shall do as you order, but you are a tyrant, miss."

"I am indeed," said Gillian, and she and Bain assisted the baronet up the stairs and into bed.

"I think you had better rest for a while, Papa. I shall

come back in a little while to see how you are doing."

Sir Hewitt's servant had followed them upstairs. He whispered something to Gillian.

"Moffat says the doctor wishes you to take this medicine, and take it you shall."

"I'll not take his damned poisons."

"You will, sir."

Sir Hewitt was immediately cowed by Gillian's imperious tone and meekly took the medicine, although muttering under his breath, "Female tyrant."

Bain and Gillian retired downstairs and sat down. "He was improving this week. I did not expect him to be worse," said Gillian, now quite worried.

"I'm sure he will be better tomorrow." He looked over at her. "You really care for him, don't you?"

"I do." She smiled. "I suppose it started as duty, but as I have grown to know him better, I found I liked him more and more. Oh, I know they say terrible things about him, and perhaps some of it is true. I really don't know. But he has much good in him if one takes the trouble to find it. I think sometimes that, had Mama met him first, before she met Lord Ashley and they had married, life would have been very different."

"If your mother was anything like you, I think you are right."

Bain's words took her by surprise, and she was about to reply when there was a pounding at the door. Moffat rushed to open it. "Stand aside. I want to see Gambol!"

Two men rushed into the room and, seeing the earl and Gillian, looked somewhat confused.

"Where is Sir Hewitt Gambol?"

The earl stood up to all his considerable height and adopted a haughty aristocratic pose. "Who are you and why have you barged into this house in such a manner?"

Impressed by his lordship's noble bearing and obviously expensive clothes, the men became politer.

"Beg your pardon, sir, but we have business with Sir Hewitt on a matter of a certain debt what's owed my employer."

"I am afraid that you will not be able to see Sir Hewitt today. He is ill and is now resting."

"We've been trying to see him for days, sir, and it is a matter of some urgency." The man's sense of mission made him bolder, "And who might I have the honor of addressing, sir?"

"I am the Earl of Bain."

"Indeed? Well, my lord, I don't want to be disturbing your lordship, but if we might see Sir Hewitt for a brief moment."

"I have said that is impossible. I suggest you and your colleague leave at once."

"No, wait, Lord Bain." Gillian stood up. "I am Sir Hewitt's daughter and you may tell me about this debt."

"You're his daughter, ma'am? Well, that does make a difference."

"Be brief, man."

"I will, your lordship. You see, ma'am, your father has debts to my employer in the amount of twelve hundred and seventy-five pounds."

"Twelve hundred and seventy-five?" repeated Gillian, startled by the amount.

"And that's only to my employer Mr. Gregson. He's more debts than that, ma'am, much more. I don't wish to worry you, but if nothing is paid very soon, I might add, Sir Hewitt might have to answer to the authorities."

"You've said what you've come to say. I suggest you leave."

"Right you are, my lord." Since the earl was glowering at them, the two men did not wish to linger. They hurried out the door.

"Oh, Bain, did you hear that? My father is in terrible trouble. I had always thought his was a very substantial fortune. He should not be going into debt for me. He paid Meg a great deal of money for my clothes and things, and then he sent me those emeralds."

"I am sure he was in debt long before he ever met you, Gillian."

"But I did not help his situation. There must be something I can do."

"I don't think it is your place to do anything, Gillian."

"But he is my father. Do you think I can allow him to go to jail?"

"I want you to do nothing until I make some inquiries myself about the matter."

"Would you do that, my lord?"

The earl smiled. "Of course, I shall do what I can."

"Thank you. Oh, dear, I do not want to distress my father by telling him about those men."

"There is no need to say anything right now. I doubt those fellows will return very soon."

Gillian seemed very disturbed and Bain silently cursed Sir Hewitt for his extravagance. He had assumed the baronet had had some money that he could one day leave to his daughter. But no, it seemed that Sir Hewitt Gambol had lost his considerable fortune. Bain thought suddenly of the large sum he had squandered at the gaming tables during the past two weeks. Were he to keep up that sort of wasteful expenditure, even he, who had one of England's largest fortunes, could end up like Sir Hewitt. This was a most sobering thought, and his lordship was a bit more charitable in his attitude toward Sir Hewitt.

thirteen

Lady Ashley stared sullenly at the young woman who stood before her. Dressed in a plain brown dress and obviously ill-at-ease, the young woman looked imploringly at her ladyship. "But I don't know what it is your ladyship expects me to find."

"I expect you to find out everything there is to know about Miss Gillian Ashley."

"She is a very nice young lady."

"I don't want a character reference, my girl. Use your brain, if God gave you one, which I am beginning to doubt."

Christobel Stourbridge was a little afraid that her mother had intimidated the young woman too much. "Don't be afraid to speak up, Kate. We simply wish to know about Miss Ashley. Whom she sees, where she goes. Everything you have observed. We are especially interested in anything out of the ordinary."

"Well, madam, there ain't much what I can see as yet. Miss goes out to parties and such and receives many callers along with the mistress. There's plenty of gentlemen coming out, suitors I should call them."

"Can you name any of these suitors?"

"Aye, m'lady. I made it a point to find out the names. There was a Mr. Thornbury and a Mr. McBride and then a

Sir Richard Thorpe. And there are others, too. Mr. Whitfield, Mr. Cavendish, Lord Ronald Swope.''

''Good gracious, Mama,'' said Christobel. ''Half of the eligible men in London have been calling on the wretched girl.''

''And Lord Renville has called several times. Mrs. James, that's the cook, has said his lordship is quite taken with Miss Ashley and she'll more than like to be a duchess one day.''

''Is there nothing more you have discovered?'' Lady Ashley was growing impatient.

''No, m'lady, but I'll keep me eyes open, your ladyship can be certain of that.''

''All right. You may go, but report to me whenever you see or hear anything of interest.''

The young woman curtsied and left. ''By all that is holy, Christobel, the girl is an idiot. Didn't Meg Fairfax have any other servants you could bribe?''

''Really, Mama, I do not like the word 'bribe' overmuch. And it seems Lady Fairfax does not have many new servants. Most of them have been with her for ages and they are disgustingly happy in her employ. I shouldn't wonder at what she pays them.''

''Well, witless as this Kate is, she did provide us with some information. Now we know this Gillian has more suitors than all the rest of the girls in London combined.''

Christobel frowned. ''Can you imagine? What they see in her I do not know. I will concede she is not so ill-looking, but she has the manners of a ruffian. You don't think Renville could be serious about her, do you? I could not bear the thought of her being a duchess. And were she to wed him, I don't think there would be any way we would keep Father from finding out about her. The marriage of the Duke of Welbourne's heir is a very important occasion.''

''Yes, it would never do at all.'' Lady Ashley got up

from her chair and began to pace the room. "Why did this wretched creature have to turn up now? It is surely the most unlucky occurrence. But still, there must be something that can be done. Perhaps she will marry young Whitfield. Isn't he the one with the estate in the West Indies? That would solve our problems, for her to go off to some accursed island."

"I doubt we shall be so lucky, Mama. But don't worry, I will not rest until I pay her back for striking me. I will find a way to ruin her, I swear it."

Lady Ashley noted her daughter's resolute expression and, knowing Christobel's stubbornness, did not doubt that somehow she would succeed.

Gillian entered Sir Hewitt's bedroom and found the baronet sitting up in bed reading the newspaper. "Oh, you are looking far better than yesterday, Papa."

Sir Hewitt grinned. "I'm feeling better. This dashed leg is a good site improved."

"You see? The doctor did help."

"Doctor? Damnation, woman, it was none of his doing. No, indeed. That idiot had nothing to do with it. The fellow would sooner see me in my grave."

Gillian pulled up a small armchair and sat down beside Sir Hewitt. She glanced at the wall over the head of his bed and noticed a small portrait of a young man with a pale complexion and large brown eyes.

"Who is that, Papa? I didn't notice it before."

"Who is it? Good heavens, you mean you say you don't know?"

"I do not. He is a very nice-looking young man."

Sir Hewitt's corpulent face took on a hurt expression. "I'd never have thought a Gambol would not recognize King Charles the Third."

"King Charles the Third? You don't mean Bonnie Prince Charlie, the young pretender?" Gillian regarded the portrait curiously. "Oh, I have seen his picture in Edinburgh, of course."

"The young pretender you say! Listen here, my girl, Charles Edward Stuart was no pretender but the rightful heir to the throne of this kingdom."

"But Papa, Bonnie Prince Charlie's cause was lost before you were even born."

"That does not signify in the least! I'll not give up my allegiance to the house of Stuart."

"Calm yourself, Papa. Your devotion is admirable, but I do hope you keep such opinions to yourself. The current royal family is very well established, and there are certain persons in the kingdom who would think your sentiments somewhat treasonous."

"Treasonous?" Sir Hewitt shook his head grimly. "They're naught but traitors, those who support the house of Hanover."

Gillian thought it best to change the subject away from the baronet's rather unusual political ideas. "Papa, I did wish to ask you something."

"My permission to marry, I'll warrant. Who is the fellow and why has he not come to see me about this?"

"No, indeed, it is not that at all," said Gillian hastily. "It is about something that happened yesterday when Lord Bain and myself were downstairs. I would have mentioned it later, but I did not want to upset you."

"What is it, daughter?"

"Two men came here yesterday. They came in and demanded to see you. Lord Bain and I would not permit it."

"Good for you! I'll not have those damned rogues in my house."

"Then you know who they were?"

"I've some idea."

"They said you owed them money. Twelve hundred and seventy-five pounds!"

"Balderdash! They're liars and knaves!"

"Then you don't owe the money?"

"Well, I might, but I don't bother about such things. A gentleman don't bother about money."

"But, Papa, this could be very serious."

"It is nothing for you to worry about. Your old papa is a wealthy man. There's no need to make a fuss about anything."

"Then perhaps you could pay these men."

"Oh, very well, I'll see them paid, the damned villains. But let's have no more about this business. Not another word. I wish to talk of more important things—your wedding, for example."

"You are impossible."

"Come now, my girl, tell me of your suitors. You must have met some young man you fancy."

"Really, Papa."

"Come, out with their names."

"I have not had any offers, if that is what you are wondering. Oh, very well, I have had a few callers, but there is no one who is serious and no one whom I would wish to consider. Indeed, I am in no rush to marry. A woman must be very careful in choosing a husband. Her entire future happiness depends on it."

"True, very true," muttered Sir Hewitt, realizing that Gillian was thinking about her mother.

"Mr. Whitfield is a very nice gentleman."

"Whitfield? Not of the Gloucestershire Whitfields?"

"I think so, yes."

"Then he is off the list. There is bad blood in that family."

Gillian grinned. "Is there, indeed? Thank you for warning me. Very well, Mr. Whitfield is off the list. Then there is Lord Ronald Swope."

"Lord Ronald Swope? By the horned god, girl, stay clear of that one. I knew his father well. One of my closest friends, in fact."

"Then, why are you against his son?"

"Would I trust my daughter to the son of a man who had the poor judgment to be a friend of mine? No, indeed!"

Gillian burst out into laughter. "You are quite ridiculous."

"There must be some other gentlemen."

"There is Lord Renville. He is a very charming young man and has been very attentive to me."

"Renville? You mean Welbourne's heir?" Gillian nodded. "Not a bad match, I suppose. You'd do well as a duchess."

"I do not think there is much chance of Renville offering for me, and even if he did, I don't know if I'd accept him. He is a nice young man, but I do not think we are well suited."

"I can see you are a particular young lady, but then I was a very particular young man in my day. We Gambols do not settle for just anyone. But you have not mentioned Oliver Bain."

"Bain?"

"Why, certainly. Now there is a young man I could tolerate. You know I won one hundred guineas by betting on him."

"You have said that, Papa."

Sir Hewitt nodded. "There's a man after my own heart. Not one of these fancy gentlemen they have about town these days. No, indeed—Bain is a fine fellow. You know, he reminds me of myself when young. He could use a wife like you, and I can tell you are not averse to the idea."

Gillian blushed. "Now, Papa, Lord Bain and I are friends and I am fond of him, but he thinks of me as a child."

"He's not such a fool as that. He's mad about you."

"My dear Papa, if you do not cease this outrageous talk, I shall leave."

Sir Hewitt Gambol grinned and did not look in the least contrite.

fourteen

"Oh, my dear, I am completely exhausted." Lady Meg Fairfax sat down on the sofa and sighed. "If we have any more callers this afternoon, I shall scream. I do not know whether I shall be able to face Lord D'Arcy's dinner party this evening. I would rather stay at home. And did you hear this news, Gillian?" Her ladyship held up a sheet of paper. "It is from Fairfax. He says he had some problem with the lambing at Riddlesea and will stay a fortnight longer in the country. I am losing all patience with the man. If I did not know him better, I should think he had a mistress in Riddlesea. Gillian? I daresay you have not heard a thing I've said."

"I am sorry, Meg." Gillian was sitting in a chair near Lady Fairfax, absently studying her embroidery. "I was thinking of my father. My visits to him lately have been rather unsettling."

"I shouldn't wonder at that, considering it is Sir Hewitt Gambol you are speaking of. Oh, I am sorry, Gillian, I know I shouldn't say anything about him. He is your papa and he is not well. I shall be more charitable in the future. But what is wrong? I thought you said he was improved since yesterday."

"Oh, yes, his leg seems improved, but I am worried

about another matter. You remember that I told you how those men came when Bain and I were there?''

"I do indeed, and speaking of Bain, I hope my cousin deigns to call upon us soon or he shall incur my wrath. But you were saying?''

"Today I asked my father if he was in financial difficulty and he denied it. He said he had enough money and would pay the debt.''

"Then that is good news.''

"But I'm not so sure it is the truth. I think he has little of his fortune left. He is not a well man and could not bear having to leave his house, and one of the men mentioned jail. Surely they could not do that to him.''

"I should not think so. But, my dear, he has paid me for your dresses and he has given you those lovely emeralds. Surely an impoverished man could not do so.''

"I hope you are right.''

"I am certain of it. Oh, dear, do I hear someone else at the door? I shall say we are indisposed.''

However, when the butler arrived in the drawing room and informed her ladyship that the identity of the caller was the Earl of Bain, Lady Fairfax was delighted. When Bain entered the room, she embraced him and then chided him harshly. "How could you stay away so long, Oliver?''

The earl shrugged. "I am sorry, Meg, but I got very involved in business matters.'' He exchanged a knowing glance with Gillian, which Meg did not notice.

"I hope for your sake those business matters do not refer to a new light skirt. Don't look shocked. I know you very well, my dear cousin. But sit down. I suppose I must forgive you, but you had best not stay away for so long again.''

"I stand rebuked.'' His lordship lowered his large frame into a chair beside Gillian. "Good day, Miss Ashley.''

"Good day, Lord Bain.''

"My heavens, you two are still so very formal. Although I imagine Gillian feels she must afford you a certain amount of deference because of your illustrious rank and advancing age."

"Really, Meg, you are being extremely vicious."

"I am still not over my annoyance with you, Oliver."

"Then I shall talk to Miss Ashley. I have made some inquiries about Sir Hewitt. It seems that he is heavily in debt."

"I knew it," Gillian shook her head. "And he has gone even further in debt because of me."

"You cannot blame yourself, my dear," said Meg. "He has not been ungenerous to you, but what he has spent is hardly enough to put a man with even a moderate fortune in debt. You must remember that Sir Hewitt has never had a reputation for being a moderate man, and I shouldn't doubt that he has had large debts for years. Although I don't know why no one has ever said anything about it."

"I don't mean to say that he is totally without assets," added his lordship. "My solicitor has made some discreet inquiries, and according to certain of his colleagues, Sir Hewitt still has some profitable lands in Devon."

"There. You see, Gillian, he is not completely destitute."

Gillian looked hopefully at Bain. "Then something can be done?"

Bain nodded. "He is in very deep trouble, but it is not hopeless by any means."

Lady Fairfax was about to add some comforting words of her own, but her butler entered the room. "I beg your pardon, my lady, but there is a problem in the kitchen that needs your ladyship's personal attention."

"Good heavens." Meg was not at all eager to leave this very interesting discussion. "Oh, very well, Hull. I shall be back shortly. You stay put, Oliver. I shall not forgive you if you run off."

After being assured by her cousin that he would remain until her return, her ladyship left them and followed the butler out.

"There must be something I can do," said Gillian, turning her large blue eyes upon the earl.

Bain found himself strangely disconcerted but managed to reply. "No, Gillian, I don't think there is anything you can do. There are very large sums of money involved."

"But I could sell my emeralds."

"I don't think that would bring enough to make much difference."

"Then what is to be done?"

Bain looked thoughtful. "Perhaps I might talk to Sir Hewitt. If he will confide in me and give me all the facts concerning these debts, perhaps I could help. That is, perhaps my solicitor could suggest something. He is a dashed clever fellow, and if there is a way for Sir Hewitt to extricate himself from these difficulties, he should discover it."

Gillian smiled gratefully at the earl. "That would be so very kind of you, Bain. I know my father respects you, and speaking to a man of sense may help."

"A man of sense?" Bain grinned. "There are many who would doubt the appropriateness of that description. My mother, for one." The mention of his mother seemed to transform the earl's mood and Gillian noted the sudden switch to melancholy.

"You have not seen her, then? I had thought she might have called."

"My mother call upon me? My dear Gillian, I doubt that would ever happen. She expects me to appear on her doorstep and wait meekly to hear if she will condescend to see me. But no, I do not intend to call upon her. I do not doubt that we have seen the last of each other for some time, which is for the best. Oh, perhaps she will come round in time, but I am not so sure that I care."

"I am so sorry."

Bain smiled. "I appreciate your concern, but there is no need to worry about me. Some sons are far better off keeping their mothers at a good distance."

"And now what are you two talking about?" Meg Fairfax returned and sat down. "I hope I didn't miss anything very interesting."

"I was just telling Miss Ashley about my new horses, four grays, perfectly matched."

Lady Fairfax turned her eyes to the heavens. "Oh, good gracious, Oliver, is that all you men ever talk about? Horses? I am sick to death of them. Oh, I am as fond of horses as the next person, but why this obsession with the creatures? But no one is worse than Fairfax." She looked over at Gillian. "You will discover that, my dear, if the man ever comes to town."

"What?" said Bain. "I thought he was arriving any day."

"Oh, that husband of mine is the most difficult man. He sent me such a dreadful letter all about lambs and some dreadful fellow who helps him about the Riddlesea estate. Now, I will suffer conversation about horses, but I do not care one whit about lambs. They are such silly little creatures always, bleating and baaing and behaving in such a stupid fashion. No, my dears, I will discuss lambs with no one and I shall make that very plain to Fairfax."

"Well, cousin, if we cannot discuss sheep, I don't see what we can discuss. I fear I must be going."

"Oliver! Don't be ridiculous. You have just arrived."

The earl rose despite her protests. "I am sorry, but I have some other appointments. Good day, Meg, Miss Ashley."

Lady Fairfax looked quite insulted, but no amount of coaxing could get her cousin to stay. When he had gone, Meg shook her head. "Can you imagine? He stays away from us for a fortnight and then stays but twenty minutes? Why, that is unbelievable. I am quite put out with him."

"Perhaps he had some other visits to make. It is growing rather late."

"Well, I do not like it. If I hear that he has deserted us for some vulgar actress, I shall be furious."

Gillian found this possibility not at all to her liking. "Do you think that is why he left? An actress?"

"My dear, you know how men are, or perhaps you don't. In any case, they can be quite trying. It is all the rage to take up with some pretty actress or dancer." Meg leaned closer to Gillian, as if she had a secret to impart. "Bain has not exactly been a monk, you know."

Gillian hoped she wasn't blushing and tried to reply with sophisticated unconcern. "I suppose that is how gentlemen are."

Meg nodded. "That is how most of them are. My Fairfax, praise God, is an exception, and should I ever hear that he ceases to be, I would probably murder him. But that Oliver. Imagine boring you with talk about his horses. I worry about him sometimes. Oh, well, I believe it is time I retired to my rooms. I have a letter I really must write. I want Fairfax to know how unhappy I am that he has broken his promise to come to town in time for Alice Lythway's party. Now we shall have to go alone. Will you excuse me, my dear? I do not like to leave you sitting by yourself."

Gillian assured her ladyship that she did not mind in the least and, after sitting for a time, went to her room.

"Can I help ye with anything, miss?" Mary MacDonald entered the room looking neat and efficient in her starched apron and cap.

"Could you fetch my emerald necklace, Mary?"

"Aye, miss. I'll ask Mr. Hull for it. 'Tis locked away with her ladyship's jewels."

The maid went off and returned a short while later. "Och, miss, Mr. Hull thinks I'm a mutton-headed girl. Ye should have heard him telling me tae be careful, not tae drop them and not tae lose them. Ye would hae thought I was taking them a thousand miles." Mary handed the box to Gillian, who opened it and was, as always, somewhat staggered by their beauty.

"Will that be all, miss?"

"There is one more thing, Mary. Do you know of any places in London that buy jewels such as this?"

"Buy them, miss? Ye're nae thinking o' selling the necklace?" Mary MacDonald immediately realized that her shocked reaction was rather impertinent, but Gillian did not seem to mind.

"I am indeed. But, Mary, I do not wish anyone to know about it. I know you can keep a secret."

"Aye, miss. I'll nae tell a soul. The only place I could say would be the Bancroft establishment. I heard Mr. Hull say that is a fine establishment and I once heard o' a lady who sold all her jewels there."

"I am fortunate you are so well-informed, Mary." She closed the box and handed it back to Mary. "Please return it to Mr. Hull. I shall soon decide what must be done."

The maid made a quick curtsy and departed, and Gillian sighed. Perhaps her necklace would not bring much, but it would help somewhat. Perhaps it would settle the most pressing of debts. In any case she could not keep the necklace knowing how much Sir Hewitt needed money. "Poor Papa," she said aloud. "I must help him somehow." Gillian walked over to the window and stared out and was soon lost in thought.

At the doorway of her room, a diminutive form lingered. Lady Fairfax's parlor maid Kate had heard every word of Gillian's conversation with Mary and had only narrowly escaped detection when Mary left the room with the necklace. Kate strained to hear anything further, but was soon convinced nothing more would be discovered by remaining any longer. She smiled happily and then went downstairs.

fifteen

Lord Bain found Sir Hewitt Gambol sitting in his favorite chair reading a book. He seemed very happy to see the earl and tossed his book aside. "Ah, Bain? What, you've come alone? No, that's right. Gillian said she wouldn't be able to call today. She has some party she must go to. Damn, I miss her even for one day. I've grown damned fond of the little minx. Well, sit down, Bain. Your pardon for not rising. This accursed gout, you see."

His lordship was rather amused by the stream of words that came from the baronet. He sat down and waited for an opportunity to speak. "I would like to discuss a certain delicate matter with you, Gambol."

Sir Hewitt regarded him curiously for a moment and then grinned. "Damn me if you ain't a quick one, Bain. I can't say I didn't expect this, but I didn't expect it so soon. Out with it, then, man."

The earl looked startled. "Out with what?"

"Dammit, Bain. I thought you were a blunt man. If you wish to ask for my daughter's hand, just come out and say it."

Bain's dark eyebrows arched in surprise. "I fear there is some mistake."

"What? You don't wish to ask for Gillian's hand?" Sir Hewitt seemed incredulous.

"That was not my purpose in coming here."

"Then you don't intend to marry Gillian? God in heaven, if your intentions are not honorable toward my daughter, you shall answer to me, sir. By God, I shall see you upon the field of honor." Sir Hewitt was growing very red-faced and the prospect of facing him in a duel seemed very ludicrous and yet somehow alarming.

"Gambol, I pray you calm down. I have only the highest esteem for Miss Ashley. On my word as a gentleman I have never harbored any dishonorable thoughts toward that young lady."

"You haven't? Good God! What sort of a man are you? She's a damned pretty girl."

Although his lordship had never before doubted his courage, he felt an urge to run from the room. Instead, he remained seated and replied very calmly. "I am endeavoring to explain to you. I have no intention of marrying anyone. And if I did bear some . . . affection toward Gillian, I should not be so foolish as to let her know it. She looks upon me like an elder brother or uncle. She is a very beautiful young lady and she has many suitors. Indeed, I know she has received visits from young Renville many times. I have heard that he is quite besotted with her and he is young, handsome, and the heir to a dukedom."

"By the great hound, I had not taken you for a fool, but I see you are a proper gudgeon and blind, too. Gillian looks upon you like a brother? She does not! I know that for a fact. I will tell you, sir, that Gillian loves you, and not as a sister loves a brother."

"That is utter nonsense. You cannot say she has told you that."

"Of course not. Would she be blabbering such things

about, even to her own papa? But I saw her face when I told her you were mad about her.''

"You told her what?''

"You heard me. Do you deny that you love her?''

Lord Bain had never before been in such a state of utter confusion.

"See? You do not deny it. I tell you, Bain. I liked you. Thought you a man after my own heart. I thought you the man for Gillian. Not a young fop like Renville. Hellfire, I don't want her to have anything to do with Renville or his kind. No, sir, I thought you were the man. Now I don't know what to think.''

Sir Hewitt scowled and glanced over at a cutlass and brace of pistols that adorned his wainscoted wall, and for a moment the earl feared the baronet intended to hop over and obtain a weapon. However, Sir Hewitt only looked at him and frowned. "If you didn't come here to ask for my daughter's hand, what did you come here for?''

"It was about your debts.''

"My debts? What business is that of yours?''

"Your daughter is very worried about you. I thought that I might be able to assist you in some way. I have a damned fine man working for me, a solicitor who is a veritable wizard with finances. I should be glad to loan you his services. Allow him to go over your financial record. He may be able to help you deal with your problems.''

"I have no need for solicitors riffling through my personal affairs. I'll thank you to mind your own business, sir. Moffat!'' Sir Hewitt shouted for his butler and the servant appeared immediately. "Show this gentleman out!''

"I wish you would be reasonable, Sir Hewitt.''

"I'll not be reasonable where my own flesh and blood is concerned. Good day to you, sir.''

Realizing that it was fruitless to try to talk any further to the baronet, his lordship rose and with a curt nod took his leave of Sir Hewitt. As he entered his carriage, the earl realized that it had been most injudicious to come here. He sat back in the seat and shouted for the driver to go on. As the vehicle clattered off he began to think. Could there be any truth of what Sir Hewitt had said? Could Gillian be in love with him? Bain dismissed the idea as absurd. Sir Hewitt was simply raving. She had given him no sign of any feelings any deeper than sisterly affection. His lordship smiled ruefully. No, Sir Hewitt was very very wrong. The earl glanced out the carriage window and thought that Sir Hewitt was not entirely wrong. His own feelings regarding Miss Ashley were definitely not brotherly.

Kate Porter knocked at the servants' entrance of Christobel Stourbridge's elegant town house and was admitted by a footman who, after realizing who she was, hastened to bring her to his mistress. Christobel and her mother were in the drawing room discussing a dinner party they would be attending that evening, but they stopped their conversation abruptly at the knowledge that the maid from Lady Fairfax's household had come to see them.

"So what do you have to tell us, Kate?" said Mrs. Stourbridge.

Kate tried hard to overcome her nervousness. "I heard something just a while ago and came right over, even though I could get in very bad trouble leaving like I did."

"Her ladyship and I realize how dedicated you are, Kate. Get to the point."

Somewhat daunted by Christobel's abruptness, the maid managed to start. "You see, madam, I heard a bit of what Lord Bain said to her ladyship and Miss Ashley. There was mention of Sir Hewitt Gambol being in debt."

"The girl is an idiot," muttered Lady Ashley. "I don't care about Sir Hewitt Gambol's debts."

"Please, Mother," said Christobel severely. "Now go on, Kate."

"Then miss went upstairs and I followed, pretending that I was polishing the furniture in the hallway. And then Mary MacDonald, lady's maid to Lady Fairfax, comes in to see Miss Ashley and I came to the door and heard every word. She said she wanted her necklace, and when Mary fetched it for her, she asked Mary if she knew any places where they might buy it."

"What sort of necklace is this?" broke in Christobel.

"Oh, madam, I saw it once. 'Tis beautiful, with emeralds. According to Mr. Hull, it is worth a fortune and the finest jewels in the house save for her ladyship's rubies. And I heard her tell Mary that she must sell the necklace and then after Mary left I heard miss say 'Poor Papa. I must help him.' "

Lady Ashley looked disgustedly at Kate and turned to Christobel. "Really, my dear, I don't see how this information can help. I really don't think the creature is capable of finding out anything that is of any consequence."

"Wait a moment, Mother. I think there is something here we can use. Allow me to think about this. Yes, I think something might be done. But it would depend on you, Kate. You have done splendidly so far. Are you willing to do more?" Since Mrs. Stourbridge accompanied this request with a gold coin, Kate nodded eagerly.

"Think of this, Mama. What would Meg Fairfax think of her guest if she found her most beloved jewels gone, stolen by this Gillian person in order to help her poor papa pay his debts?"

"That is preposterous, Christobel. As disreputable as this girl is, I daresay she will not steal Lady Fairfax's jewels."

"Of course not, Mama. But what if she takes her necklace to the jeweler and somehow one of the Fairfax heirlooms vanishes at the same time. Perhaps Kate here could take one of the necklaces and send it to the jeweler, saying it is from Gillian."

Kate had been listening in silence, but the mention of stealing Lady Fairfax's jewels made her forget her fear of Lady Ashley. "Wait a moment, madam! Stealing? No, I won't do it. I'll not end up in prison or worse."

"You silly little fool," snarled Christobel. "If you keep your wits about you, you'll run no risk."

"No, madam. The jewels is locked up tight and only Mr. Hull has the key. 'Tis too risky. No, madam, I'll not do it."

"Really, Christobel, you cannot expect this inept creature to do such a thing. She would make a mess of it. I do not think this idea has any merit at all. I suggest you come up with something better."

Christobel had never let go of an idea in her life and was not about to start now. "Surely, there is access to Meg Fairfax's jewels. Kate, I want you to listen carefully. You do not wish to take risks." Christobel smiled. "Wouldn't you be willing to take a small risk for one hundred pounds?"

"One hundred pounds?" Kate stared at Christobel in amazement. She would not see such a sum if she saved her entire salary for five years.

"One hundred pounds. What do you think?"

Kate looked from Christobel to Lady Ashley and then nodded. Christobel smiled triumphantly and began to think how the plan might work. The butler interrupted them by bringing in a letter on a silver salver.

"Why, it is addressed to you, Mama." Christobel handed the letter to her mother. "And it is from Father."

"Oh, dear," muttered Lady Ashley, taking the letter and breaking the seal. She read it quickly and her face took on an expression of extreme distaste. "I swear that man lives only to vex me."

"What is it?"

"Your father is summoning me back to the country and he requests you come, too, if your husband will allow it."

"If my husband will allow it? What has that to do with anything? Freddy allows me to do as I please, and Father knows that well enough."

"He purports to be ill. I doubt it is anything serious. You know how he is. Still, he is most definite in wishing me to return. How beastly of him, especialy with the Lythway dinner party coming up. But what can I do? I must go."

"But what of our plans?" Christobel glanced over at Kate.

"Oh, yes." Lady Ashley looked at the maid. "Would you please wait in the other room?"

Kate nodded and left. "What is it, Mama?"

"Don't you see, Christobel? This is perfect. We leave town, and whatever the dull-witted creature does, no one can blame us. Even if she were caught and said we put her up to it, we could simply deny it. We would be away at Ashley Manor."

"That is a point, Mama, but I should prefer being around to see what happens."

"You think it over, my dear. I must go and start my girl on packing." Lady Ashley left her daughter to consider the problems and possible complications of her scheme.

sixteen

L ord and Lady Twickenham had spared no pains to ensure that their ball would be the most splendid of the Season. Although Lord Twickenham was by no means the wealthiest of men, he sought to give this appearance by the magnificence of his ballroom and the great crowd of elegantly dressed ladies and gentlemen who had shown up to partake of his hospitality.

Oliver Bain was well acquainted with Lord Twickenham and did not like him in the least. The earl would have preferred to miss the ball, but a short note from his mother made this impossible. After such a long time of no word, Lady Bain sent her son a short communication stating she intended to attend the Twickenham ball and she would expect her son to escort her there. Although Bain did not much like the cold tone of this note, he was glad for the opportunity to end the feud between his mother and himself.

Vowing to be conciliatory, the earl arrived at his mother's house at the appointed hour and did his best to be agreeable. Lady Bain, however, seemed intent upon vexing him and remained cold and distant. His lordship was, therefore, glad to arrive at the Twickenham house, where he was soon able to relinquish his mother to her numerous friends and acquaintances and retreat across the room in search of more congenial company.

This he found in the person of his cousin Meg Fairfax, who was looking very glamorous in a gown of ivory silk. "Meg, how well you look."

Meg was standing with another lady with whom the earl was slighty acquainted and with a stout gentleman whom Bain knew from his club. He exchanged greetings with them both and was happy when they soon moved on, leaving him alone with his cousin.

"Oliver, I daresay I am still a bit irritated with you for running off this afternoon. I was telling Gillian that you are the most inconsiderate fellow."

"Where is Gillian?"

"Why, over there. She is wearing green. You do see her, don't you. Just look for all the gentlemen and you will find Gillian."

Bain made no reaction to this comment, but he found it irked him. He looked across the ballroom and found Gillian in the crowd. As usual, she looked lovely, and Bain saw that she was thronged with young gentlemen. "She seems very popular."

"My dear Oliver, she is a sensation. It seems that no one can resist her. I am so very thrilled for her. Of course, I am a trifle bit jealous. I scarcely created any notice my first Season."

"Nonsense, Meg. As I recall, my mama said you had no rivals."

"Your mama was being kind. By the way, where is my aunt?"

"Talking to her friends. She has a great many of them and I think she finds them all far more agreeable than me."

"Oliver, you have been quarreling again."

"Of course, Meg. When do we not quarrel?"

"Well, I think it is very sad. Look, here comes Gillian."

His lordship watched Gillian come toward them and realized that he had never seen her looking more beautiful. She smiled at him and extended her hand.

He took it and bowed. "There should be regulations against ladies looking as lovely as you, Miss Ashley. Gentlemen have no defense against such beauty."

Gillian smiled. "Bain, I should not have thought I would hear such bosh coming from you. Really!"

Meg laughed. "Oh, Oliver can be very gallant when he is in the proper mood. There are a great many ladies that can attest to that."

"Meg!"

Lady Fairfax laughed at the look her cousin gave her and turned to Gillian. "How did you escape from your admiring throng?"

"I told them I had promised Lord Bain the next dance. I hope you don't mind."

Bain smiled. "Mind? I am delighted and flattered that you would leave all your suitors. I see they are looking daggers at me."

"They are no such thing," said Gillian. "But I am so glad to see you. Everyone is being so silly and tiresome, and I am growing tired being so sweet and charming. I can be myself with you, my lord, for you know how dull and irksome I can be."

"Irksome perhaps, but hardly dull," said his lordship with a smile. The music started and the ladies and gentlemen started to waltz about the polished ballroom floor. "This is my dance, then?"

Gillian nodded and, saying farewell to Meg, took his lordship's arm and was led over to the other dancers. It was, Gillian recognized, a very pleasant sensation to find herself in Bain's arms. He was an excellent dancer, and yet Gillian realized that she would not have cared if he had been the worst dancer there.

"I saw your father this afternoon."

"You did? How was he feeling?"

"He seemed better then when I last saw him."

Gillian looked up into the earl's face as they waltzed across the room. They passed the other dancers but took no notice of anyone else. "I offered him the advice of my solicitor, but I fear he took the offer badly."

"I suppose he would. He is so awfully proud and hard-headed." Gillian smiled. "But that is the way men are, isn't it?"

He gave her a look of mock indignation. "Really, miss, you cannot expect me to listen meekly while you inpugn my sex."

"Oh, no, I suppose not." She smiled, but then grew serious. "I am worried about him, Bain."

"Sir Hewitt can take care of himself. He would not want you fretting over him."

"I know, but I can't help it. It's funny; I have known him such a short time, but I feel as if I have known him all my life. It must be because he is my father. I am so glad that I finally found him."

"I think he is very lucky to have found such a daughter, and he thinks so, too."

"Does he?"

"Of course."

They continued to dance and did not speak for a time. "I am glad to see that you were with your mother. One of the gentlemen pointed her out to me because she was standing beside his sister. She is a very handsome lady."

"We are hardly reconciled as yet."

"But you are making progress?"

"I suppose so."

"Then that is good. You must not be discouraged. You know, ladies can be nearly as stubborn as gentlemen."

Bain laughed and was about to make a reply when the music ended. His lordship had barely started to escort

Gillian back when they were besieged by young gentlemen, one of them insisting that Miss Ashley had promised him the next dance.

Gillian, who thought her dance with Bain certainly the shortest one she had ever danced, had no alternative but to graciously accede to the young gentleman's wishes.

The earl had found dancing with Gillian Ashley to be a rather disquieting experience. He realized that he was growing dangerously fond of that young lady and found himself thinking again of his conversation with Sir Hewitt Gambol. However, his lordship did not have much opportunity to reflect upon this, for he looked over and saw his mother looking at him. Standing beside her was Henrietta Colville.

Lady Bain waved at her son and his lordship found himself wishing his mother did not seem so suddenly conciliatory. However, the dowager countess was smiling and gesturing toward him, and he had no choice but to join her and her unfortunate companion.

"Oliver, Mrs. Colville and I were just discussing you."

"Indeed, Mama?" He looked over at Henrietta, who was regarding him with a curious look.

"Yes, Mrs. Colville was saying how much she and her husband enjoy your company. What a kind thing to say."

"You know, Lady Bain, that your son is my husband's closest friend."

"And where is John?" said the earl, glancing about the room.

"Oh, he is somewhere about, Bain. He is with Lord Twickenham and some other gentlemen, and they are discussing horses."

"I did wish to speak to John."

"You shall have plenty of time to see Mr. Colville, Oliver. Mrs. Colville was saying that she seldom sees you and I daresay I think you had better pay more attention to your calls. Who was that girl you were dancing with?" His lordship was surprised by his mother's abrupt change of conversation.

"That was Gillian Ashley."

"So that is the creature." Lady Bain frowned. "Not a bad-looking girl, I will admit."

"So that is the famous Gillian?" Henrietta Colville smiled knowingly at the earl. "I have heard so much about her. She is so very popular with the young men. I suspect her appeal is due to having such a scandalous mother. I fancy the young men find such things romantic."

"Then they are very stupid," said the dowager countess testily. "The girl openly acknowledges the fact that Hewitt Gambol is her father. I find it disgraceful. I think the parents of those young gentlemen should make it very clear that they will not tolerate any familiarity with such an undesirable young woman. I intend to speak to your cousin Meg about it. I do not approve of her harboring such a person."

"Harboring such a person? Good heavens, Mother, Gillian Ashley is a very charming young lady and her appeal to the young men is obvious to me. There is scarcely another young lady in London as pretty or charming, and hers is a genuine charm, not in the least artificial."

"Why, Bain," said Henrietta Colville, "it sounds as if you are enamored of her."

"Don't be absurd."

Henrietta Colville smiled benignly at him, but was in truth exceedingly irritated. So this was the reason the earl had been so indifferent toward her. It seemed he had his eye on this dark-haired Gillian. Henrietta glanced over at Gillian and wondered how his lordship could prefer the girl to herself. "She is really quite wild, you know, Lady Bain."

"Wild, Mrs. Colville?"

"Oh, haven't you heard how she provoked an argument

with Mrs. Stourbridge and then struck her across the face?''

''Indeed!'' said Lady Bain. ''Oliver, what do you know of this?''

''I have not heard anything about it and suspect the story is the product of someone's imagination.''

''You are very quick to come to her defense, Oliver.'' The dowager countess regarded her son suspiciously.

Bain started to make an indignant reply, but checked himself. ''I do hope you ladies will excuse me. I have not seen John for some time and would like to find him.'' The earl bowed rather stiffly and left them.

Henrietta Colville shook her head and spoke in a confidential tone. ''I fear, Lady Bain, that your son has lost his heart. Perhaps it is not so surprising. She is a rather pretty girl.'' Henrietta paused and then continued. ''And perhaps it is time for Bain to marry. I was just speaking of that to my husband.''

''Marry? You don't think that has crossed his mind? My dear Mrs. Colville, this Gillian person is totally unacceptable. Surely my son knows that no one like her could ever be Countess of Bain.''

''I should hope so, Lady Bain, although it seems a great many gentleman have fallen under her spell.'' Henrietta directed her gaze toward Gillian. ''Look at that. Young Renville has joined her. It is very clear he is very interested. I have heard that his mother the duchess is very upset about the attention he is paying her.''

''I do not blame the duchess. It is most alarming to think of someone with this girl's background becoming one's daughter-in-law.'' Lady Bain cast a disapproving gaze at Gillian. ''I should like to meet this girl.''

''You would?''

The dowager nodded. ''I must admit I am very curious about her.''

''Then I shall arrange it. I know young Renville very

well. He is a good friend of my husband's brother. I shall have him introduce us."

"I would prefer you brought the young woman to me."

"Oh, that will not be difficult. Wait here, Lady Bain."

Henrietta was very eager to meet Gillian Ashley. Obviously Bain preferred the girl to herself, and Mrs. Colville wanted to find out why. She made her way across the room toward Gillian.

Gillian thought Lord Renville a nice young man, but she always found his conversation quite uninteresting. Young Renville could talk at length on only two subjects—horses and hounds—and since Gillian had never hunted, she never had much to say on the subjects. Renville was content to monopolize the conversation and regaled her with what he considered to be very amusing anecdotes.

Gillian was therefore not at all unhappy to be interrupted by the arrival of another lady. She looked at Henrietta Colville and smiled, not knowing who this attractive lady might be. Gillian saw that she was known to Renville, for that gentleman looked up and greeted her.

"Mrs. Colville, how good to see you."

"Good evening, Renville. I do hope you will be so kind as to introduce me to this lady. I am eager to meet her."

"Of course. Mrs. Colville, may I present Miss Ashley. Miss Ashley, this is Mrs. Colville. You have heard me speak of my friend William. He owns the fine bay hunter I was just speaking about. Mrs. Colville is his sister-in-law."

Gillian nodded politely. "How do you do, Mrs. Colville?"

"I am very well indeed," said Henrietta sweetly. She then turned to Renville. "I was just talking to Lady Bain and she said that young gentlemen have monopolized Miss Ashley all evening. She would dearly love to meet you, Miss Ashley, and I have told her I would endeavor to bring you to her. I hope you will come. I know Renville will excuse us.''

Renville did not look too eager to do so. "Have pity, Mrs. Colville, I have had little time with Miss Ashley and she has promised me this dance.''

The music was starting and Renville looked imploringly at Henrietta, who ignored him. "Men have no consideration. Poor Miss Ashley has been dancing all night. I know she will appreciate a relaxing talk with some ladies. Be a good lad, Renville, and go find someone else to talk to.''

Renville looked resentfully at Henrietta but had little choice but to take his leave. Gillian, curious as she was about meeting Bain's mother, found the prospect somewhat unsettling and would have much preferred Lord Renville's inexpert dancing.

"I hope you don't mind me taking you away from your dance. Lady Bain wants to meet you, since her son has told her so much about you. She is over there in the corner. Come with me.''

Gillian felt some trepidation but allowed herself to be led across the ballroom floor. She thought Mrs. Colville the most glamorous woman she had ever seen, and although her dress was rather daring, she looked splendid.

"You certainly are a triumph, Miss Ashley. It seems you have won many hearts and have been in town a very short time. I congratulate you.''

"You exaggerate, ma'am.''

"I think not.''

As they walked through the crowd, Henrietta noted Gillian's gaze seemed to fall upon someone and remain there, and looking across the ballroom, Henrietta realized Oliver Bain was the object of her scrutiny.

"Oh, you are looking at Lord Bain.''

Gillian blushed. "No . . . or yes, perhaps I am.''

"You are well acquainted with him, are you not?''

"I am staying with his cousin Lady Fairfax."

"Then you have had many opportunities to see him. He is a handsome man, Lord Bain, and he is my husband John's dearest friend. But I should caution you about losing your heart to him."

Gillian looked at Henrietta in surprise. "Do not be silly, Mrs. Colville."

"Oh, but I know how charming he can be. There is something about him that appeals to women. But if I may be frank, Miss Ashley, his tastes do not run to innocent girls just out of the schoolroom."

"Really, Mrs. Colville, I don't know why you should tell me such things."

"I only wish to spare you pain. You see, my dear, I know Bain very well." She paused. "Very well, if you get my meaning."

Gillian stopped and looked at the older woman in some confusion. Slowly she realized what Henrietta was implying.

"Yes, indeed. I thought you knew," continued Mrs. Colville. "It is generally known about town. Lord Bain and I are—how should I say it?—very closely acquainted."

Gillian regarded Henrietta in disbelief. "But you said your husband is Bain's dearest friend."

Henrietta smiled. "He is. They have known each other for ages, but John is a very understanding man. He would never grudge Bain anything, not even his wife." Henrietta laughed at Gillian's startled expression. "My poor dear, you are such an innocent."

Gillian stared at Mrs. Colville. Could it possibly be true? Meg had hinted that Bain was having an affair and Henrietta Colville was very beautiful. Perhaps she was incredibly naive.

Gillian tried to seem nonchalant. "How very interesting," she said, and continued walking.

Lady Bain was sitting in a chair in an unobtrusive corner

of the ballroom and scutinizing Gillian very carefully as she walked toward her. Not bad-looking, she thought grudgingly, and managed a gracious smile as Henrietta Colville introduced them.

"Do sit down, my dear," said the dowager countess, motioning toward the chair beside her.

Gillian did as she was bid. Henrietta started to sit down, but a stern look from the dowager countess stopped her. "I think your husband was looking for you, Mrs. Colville."

"Indeed, Lady Bain? Then I shall take leave of you ladies." Although Henrietta was eager to hear what the dowager was going to say to Gillian, she gracefully retired. As she walked away, Henrietta Colville smiled. She was certain that between her own revelation about Bain and what Lady Bain was undoubtedly going to say, this Miss Ashley could have no thought of linking herself with the earl.

Gillian found herself searching Lady Bain's countenance for some resemblance to his lordship. She found very little, for Lady Bain was pale and delicate with classically sculptured features, so unlike the earl's.

"It is good of you to spend some time with me, Miss Ashley."

"Oh, I am glad to have the opportunity to meet you, ma'am."

"That is kind of you to say, child. It seems my niece Meg Fairfax has taken quite a liking to you."

"Lady Fairfax has been so good to me. I have never met a kinder or more generous lady. I am so indebted to her."

"And it seems my son has taken an interest in you, too."

Gillian detected a sudden hostility in Lady Bain's voice and replied warily, "Lord Bain has been very considerate to me, my lady."

"How very good of him." Lady Bain frowned and

Gillian found herself growing very uncomfortable. The dowager countess continued. "I am acquainted with Lady Honoria Ashley. Are you related to her family?"

"Lady Bain, I think you are aware that my father is Sir Hewitt Gambol."

"Indeed I am, miss, but I note that you go by the name Ashley, which is rather unfortunate for the Ashley family, don't you think? I wish to tell you, miss, that if society and the Prince Regent care to accept you as respectable, that is very fortunate for you. But I tell you one thing: I will not allow my son to have anything more to do with you. He has brought me enough pain without making a fool of himself over some reprobate's ill-begotten spawn."

The awe she felt toward the formidable dowager countess vanished as Gillian grew red with anger. "You have no right to speak to me in such an infamous manner."

"I have every right. I have my son's interest at heart."

"Do you indeed? I have my doubts of that. It seems you care little for Bain's welfare."

"Whatever do you mean?"

"I mean that you have been plaguing your son ever since the death of his brother. Don't you know what you are doing to him, blaming him for his brother's death? You must know that it was not his fault! Bain is a good man who loved his brother very much. He would never have caused him harm, and yet he is in agony thinking you hold him responsible. If you care for him, you must stop making him miserable. You will destroy him if you persist."

The dowager countess gaped at Gillian, astonished at her impertinence. "How could you?" she sputtered. "How could you say such things to me? Get away from me! Get away!"

Gillian got up and hurried away. Visibly upset, she searched for Meg Fairfax and found her talking to a stout gentleman. "Meg, forgive me, but I wish to go home."

"What is wrong?" Meg was alarmed by Gillian's expression.

"Are you unwell?" said the stout gentleman, eyeing her with interest.

"No . . . yes. Oh, please, Meg, may I speak to you?"

"Yes, of course, my dear. Would you excuse us?" Meg asked the stout gentleman, who nodded and walked off. "Now, what is this about, Gillian?"

"Oh, Meg, I had a row with Lady Bain!"

"A row?"

"She said terrible things to me and I lost my temper. She was very angry. Oh, Meg, what will Bain think of me?"

"I don't think you should worry about that. He knows my aunt can be the most horrible woman. Really, Gillian, you must try and keep this temper of yours in check. One should try not to offend my aunt, insufferable as she is. But it is done and you must not upset yourself over it."

"Please, Meg, I wish to go home."

Although Meg thought it better that they stay, she saw that Gillian was in no mood to do so. "Very well," she said, and the two of them made their way out of the ballroom.

Bain was quite alarmed at the condition in which he found his mother. The usually imperturbable countess was sitting in the chair, dabbing at her eyes with her handkerchief.

"Mother, whatever is the matter?"

"I shall never forgive you, Oliver. That creature! That insufferable creature!"

"Whom are you talking about?"

"I am talking about that wretched, vulgar Gillian Ashley. Why must you disparage me to her?"

"What do you mean?"

"It seems you have told her I am a monster, that I make you miserable. I, your own mother! You told her I blame you for Edgar's death. Oh, Oliver, how could you tell her such things? How could you discuss family matters with that . . . person?''

"Mother, calm down. You are distraught!"

"And with good reason. I tell you this, Oliver: if you ever again exchange as much as one word with this creature, I shall never speak to you again. Can you imagine the shock of hearing the wretched girl say these things to me?''

"Come, I'll take you home."

"You will do no such thing." The countess stood up and regarded her son angrily. "I will not ride in the same carriage with you. I shall ask someone else to take me home. Please leave me."

Bain protested, but the dowager was adamant. "Very well, Mother," he said stiffly. "I will do as you wish." He turned and walked briskly away. Confound it, he thought. What had come over Gillian? Bain's eyes searched the ballroom, but Gillian was not there. He must find her and discover what had transpired between her and the dowager.

"Looking for someone, Bain?"

The earl turned to face Henrietta Colville.

She smiled. "If you are looking for Miss Ashley, I saw her and Meg Fairfax leave a few minutes ago."

Bain did not reply to her but rushed off. He had to find Gillian. When he arrived outside, he hurried to his carriage and shouted to his startled driver to move over. Taking up the reins himself, he whipped his horses into action.

His lordship maneuvered his horses through the dark streets with practiced skill and arrived at Meg Fairfax's house just as Meg and Gillian were walking into the house. Tossing the reins to his driver, he jumped down from the vehicle. "Gillian!" he shouted.

Hearing his shout, Meg and Gillian turned to see him bound up the walk after them.

"Oliver, is that you?"

"Yes, Meg, I want to talk to Gillian."

"Very well, Oliver, but let us not stand out here on the street. Come inside."

Once inside the drawing room, Gillian looked over at the earl's face. She could see he was very angry and she felt herself trembling.

"Gillian, I want to know what happened between you and my mother."

"Bain, I lost my temper. I am sorry I did so, but she said some terrible things to me."

"I can well believe it, Oliver," said Meg. "I know my aunt."

"I pray you, Meg, allow Gillian to speak. I want to know exactly what you said to her."

"I said that she was hurting you by blaming you for your brother's death. I told her she must stop making you miserable."

"God in heaven, Gillian! You had no right to say anything of the kind to her. What I have said to you was in confidence. What is between my mother and myself is a family matter, and no one else has any right to interfere."

"I am sorry, Bain, but I was provoked beyond endurance."

"Provoked beyond endurance? Just as you were provoked to strike Mrs. Stourbridge? Oh, yes, I heard about that and I had thought it was nonsense. Now I do not doubt it is true."

"Oliver," interjected Meg. "Perhaps Gillian did slap Christobel Stourbridge. But she said the vilest things. I was there, Oliver, and I admired Gillian's restraint."

"Well, I do not. A lady does not behave in such a manner. And no matter what my mother said, there is no excuse for betraying my confidence. Dammit, Gillian, don't you realize what harm you have done?"

"But—"

"There can be no excuses! You have betrayed my trust."

"Oliver!" cried Meg. "You cannot be angry with Gillian. Your mother was definitely at fault. But Gillian will send an apology to your mother if that will make you happy."

"I don't think she deserves one," Gillian said, looking defiantly at Bain.

"What?" Bain regarded Gillian in surprise. "You're not sorry for what you said to her?"

"I am sorry that you are angry, but I am not sorry for telling her the truth. She was horrible to me! Her rank does not entitle her to behave in such a way. No, Bain, I am not sorry at all!"

The earl and Gillian exchanged angry looks, and Meg stepped between them. "Oliver, I think you had best go home. There is no point in speaking any more of this tonight. We are all very tired. You must both have time to cool down."

Bain looked coldly at Gillian and then turned to Meg. "Perhaps you are right, Meg. I had best go home." Without another word, he left them. He would go home and get drunk and the devil take everyone.

Gillian begged Meg to say nothing further and retired to her room. After a brave showing before Mary MacDonald, who helped her to undress, Gillian fell upon her bed and cried herself to sleep.

seventeen

G illian did not sleep very well and awoke feeling restless and unhappy. She kept going over her words with Bain and remembering his expression and hurt and anger. As if this were not bad enough, she could not keep from thinking about Henrietta Colville. She was not quite sure that Henrietta was Bain's mistress. Gillian buried her head in the pillow. What did it matter anyway? Bain could never care for her now. Whatever affection he might have felt for her had vanished. She would probably never see him again.

These gloomy thoughts were interrupted by the appearance of Mary MacDonald, who seemed exasperatingly cheerful as she pulled open the curtains and said, "Good morning to ye, miss."

Gillian did her best to be civil and hurried to get dressed and join Meg Fairfax at breakfast. Meg had risen earlier than usual and was sitting in the dining room reading a letter.

"Oh, Gillian," she said. "Can you imagine? Another letter from my husband and yet another excuse for not coming to town. I shall have to go to Riddlesea myself and drag him here." Meg put down the letter and looked up at her guest. "Are you feeling any better?"

"I'm fine, Meg."

171

"Do help yourself to some breakfast."

"Thank you." Although she was not very hungry, Gillian made an attempt to fill her plate. She sat down beside Meg at the table and stared idly at her breakfast sausages.

"I pray you, do not be so gloomy, Gillian. I would not give one fig for my aunt's opinion. She is a difficult woman."

"I do not care about her, but Bain will never forgive me."

"Of course he will." Meg regarded Gillian curiously. "You care for my cousin, don't you? Oh, I am a goose not to have noticed it. I am usually aware of these things, but this has caught me by surprise. I thought you were developing a *tendre* for young Renville. But it is Oliver, isn't it? You are in love with him."

Gillian smiled ruefully. "I beg you say nothing to Bain. I daresay he would find it very amusing. I should feel like such a fool. I know he is in love with someone else, which is rather horrid of him, considering who it is. She is quite odious."

"Whatever do you mean?" Meg was intrigued. She had suspected her cousin of having a new mistress, for he had been acting strangely the past few weeks, but she had no clue as to the lady's identity. "Do you know the name of the lady?"

Gillian nodded.

"Then for heaven's sake, tell me."

"Henrietta Colville."

Meg's forkful of kipper stopped midway between her plate and her mouth. "You must be joking."

"I couldn't believe it at first, but now I don't know. She as much as told me so and she is very beautiful."

"Perhaps so, but that is beside the point. She is married to John Colville. He is Oliver's oldest friend."

"Mrs. Colville said her husband is very understanding

about it. I admit I am not used to such things. I expect Bain must be very much in love with her."

"I refuse to believe it. I know very well that John Colville is besotted with the dreadful woman, and were he to find this out, it would kill him. I know my cousin, and madly in love or no, he would not do anything to hurt John. She was quizzing you, my dear. Oh, that despicable woman."

Gillian made no reply but stared glumly at her plate.

"Gillian, you really can't believe that she is telling the truth?"

"I don't know what to think, Meg, but I do know one thing, and that is that I must leave London."

"But the Season has scarcely started."

"I must leave here, Meg. I cannot go on like this, pretending I am respectable and trying to snare a husband. I never really liked the idea. I am not respectable and do not belong in society."

"Now you are talking rubbish. You must stay at least until the end of the Season."

"No, if I stay longer I shall cause more trouble for you."

"You have caused me no trouble."

"But I have, Meg. I have caused you and Bain trouble, and I shall not forgive myself for doing so. My mind is made up, and there is nothing that will change my decision." Gillian stood up abruptly. "Pray excuse me, I told my father I would visit him this morning."

Gillian did not allow Meg to say another word and hurried from the dining room.

Lady Fairfax put down her fork and frowned. She reflected that it was funny how attached she had grown to Gillian in these few short weeks. Without her the Season would be hopelessly dull and the house so very empty.

Meg thought carefully. There must be something she could do to help. For one thing, she could see her aunt and talk some sense to Lady Bain. A slight smile crossed Meg's lips. It was not easy to talk sense to the dowager, nor was it easy to talk sense to the Earl of Bain.

"Good gracious," said her ladyship aloud, "she is in love with Oliver. I am a goose for not seeing it. Good heavens, she is perfect for him." Meg shook her head and reflected that she must have been blind. She had spent much time trying to think of the perfect husband for Gillian, while all the time there was no better candidate than her cousin Oliver.

Meg had many times thrown eligible ladies in Bain's way and he had never been interested. Meg stared thoughtfully across the room. There was something between him and Gillian. Yes, she thought, they were well suited in many ways.

Meg got up from her chair and started for her room. She would see what she could do about the matter, she thought; and had every confidence that she could make matters right.

Gillian's mood was lightened somewhat when she entered Sir Hewitt's house and found her father looking very much improved. The baronet was so much better that he was able to walk again with his cane, and he greeted her with a warm embrace.

"You see, my girl, I'm walking again. 'Tis all your nagging about giving up wine."

"Then you have done so, Papa?"

"Not exactly, my girl, but I've not been drunk in three weeks' time."

This curious admission made Gillian embrace her father and kiss him soundly on the cheek. "That is wonderful, Papa! And are you eating all that cook has been making?"

Sir Hewitt's elfin countenance fell. "Aye, but it is foul stuff that."

"It is good for you. Now sit down, Papa. You must not overdo."

The baronet obediently hobbled over to the sofa and sat down. "Now, my girl, I want to hear all about your ball last night. I suspect you made many conquests."

Gillian was not at all eager to discuss the ball, but smiled. "It was a very fine ball, but the Prince Regent did not appear."

"Good. I don't want you to have anything to do with that usurper to the throne."

Gillian thought it best to change the subject. "Papa, I am thinking about leaving London."

"Leaving London?" Sir Hewitt looked horrified. "You would leave your old papa?"

"No, I shouldn't want to do that, but, Papa, I thought perhaps we both could leave town. You have a home in the country."

"Crestwyck? Egad, I abominate the place."

"But I'm sure it is lovely. I adore the country and it would be the very thing for you. You'd be out in the fresh air. I know it would do wonders for you."

"Dash it all, Gillian, it would be a dreadful bore."

"But I should be there with you."

"But it would be a bore for you. You'd not be happy out there with only an old fellow like me for company. You must stay here and meet the right people. By the gods, my girl, you need a husband.

"No, don't say you don't. A woman needs a husband and I want to see you married well while I live. I thought I'd had my wish, but the rogue Bain ruined it all."

Gillian looked up at the mention of Bain's name. "Bain? What has he to do with anything?"

"Why, the fellow came to see me yesterday. I was sure he was going to ask for your hand. And I wouldn't have objected. I like the man. He reminds me a bit of myself at that age. But the fool says that was not his intention. He's come to tell me he'll loan his solicitor to me to see to my debts. Imagine the fellow's effrontery. In my days a gentleman's debts were his own affair.''

"Oh, Papa, you didn't say anything to him about asking for my hand?''

"Of course I did.''

"Oh, Papa! I shall die of embarrassment.''

"Well, he'll come round soon. He's got the idea that you don't care for him. You'll have to tell him the truth.''

"The truth?''

"That you are fond of him.''

"Really, Papa, I do not wish to discuss this any further. And I should be grateful to you if you did not say such things to Lord Bain again. Of course, I doubt if you will have any opportunity. I do not expect to be seeing much of him. And you are very much mistaken to think I am enamored of him.

"Please, Papa, I wish to leave London. Please say you will come with me somewhere.''

Sir Hewitt looked thoughtful. "Perhaps the country would be a change, but I warn you it is a damned uncomfortable old house. Oh, very well, daughter, if you wish to go to the country, why not? We shall go to Crestwyck.''

"Oh, Papa!'' Gillian threw her arms around the baronet's neck and hugged him joyfully. "You will see that it will be such fun.''

"Perhaps,'' said Sir Hewitt, pleased by Gillian's delight, "but you may change your mind once you see it. It is in Devon on the damnedest most barren land in England.''

"I know I shall love it.''

The baronet was not at all certain of this, but before he could reply, his butler came into the room. "Your pardon, sir, but that Mr. Gregson is here again.''

"Confound it, Moffat! Throw the rascal out!''

"The rascall will not be thrown out!" A stony-faced man appeared at the doorway. "I'll not be put off any longer, Gambol. I'll have my money or I'll see you in jail."

Sir Hewitt's face purpled with rage. "Damn you, Gregson! Get out of my house. Get out, I say!"

Gillian was worried for her father's health and stood up. "Please, Papa, calm yourself." She turned to Mr. Gregson. "I beg you, sir, have some care for my father's condition. He has not been well."

Mr. Gregson was somewhat disarmed by Gillian's beauty and was not unsympathetic.

"You must understand, miss, that Sir Hewitt has been avoiding payment of his debts to me for a year now. I am not a rich man, miss."

"Damn you, Gregson! You're as rich as Croesus and a damned liar."

"I've been patient too long, Gambol. I'll have my money or you will regret it very soon."

"Mr. Gregson." Gillian turned her large blue eyes upon him and spoke in a conciliatory tone. "I promise you I shall see that you get your money very soon."

"Gillian!"

"Please, Papa! You have my word, Mr. Gregson. Will you accept it?"

Mr. Gregson hesitated. "Very well, miss. Here is my card and I'll expect word soon. Good day."

The man left and Sir Hewitt shouted an oath after him.

Gillian regarded Sir Hewitt sternly. "Now, Papa, you must endeavor to pay Mr. Gregson." She glanced about the room. "What do you have that you can sell?"

"Sell? In God's name, girl, I'll not sell a thing."

"You must! This man is serious. Would you want your daughter to have to visit you in jail? Indeed, Papa, it is time you took affairs in hand."

"But we're going to Devon. We can leave tonight."

"We will go nowhere until Mr. Gregson is satisfied.

Now I have the emeralds you gave me; they should fetch a very high price. Perhaps they would be enough.''

"The emeralds! You wouldn't sell them.''

"They are far less important to me than you are.'' She took his hand. "I don't need expensive presents, Papa, but I do need a papa who is free from debt. Don't you understand? You must pay this man and the others. There are others, aren't there, Papa?''

Sir Hewitt nodded. "A great many.''

"Then we must start with your debt to Mr. Gregson. Have you anything else you might sell? Any other jewelry?''

Sir Hewitt frowned and then looked down at his hand. "There is my ring.''

"Good, Papa. Give it to me. I shall see to it.''

"But it won't do for a girl to be selling jewelry.''

"It will do very well. You are too unwell to go about town, and so I will do it for you. Tell me what you think the ring and the necklace will bring.''

Sir Hewitt shrugged, but could do nothing but answer his very determined daughter.

Meg Fairfax greeted Lady Bain with a kiss on the cheek. "My dear aunt, you are looking very well.''

Lady Bain did not acknowledge the compliment. She was not at all happy to see her niece. She had always thought Meg overly frivolous and the fact that she had thrust Gillian Ashley upon society was, in Lady Bain's eyes, a very grave fault.

"Do sit down, Meg. Tell me how is your husband?''

Meg sat down across from her aunt. "Oh, he is very well, but the naughty man is still at Riddlesea. He has never been fond of town and I daresay is trying to stay in the country as long as possible.''

Lady Bain frowned disapprovingly. "I do not think it

healthy for husband and wife to be separated for long periods of time. There is too much mischief afoot."

"Indeed," said Meg, repressing a smile. "I do agree. I assure you Fairfax will return shortly or I shall send guards to Riddlesea to fetch him."

The dowager countess did not find this remark amusing. "I expect you are seeing Oliver often. You and he were always so very close."

Meg nodded. "I saw him last night, of course, but I do not see him as much as I would like. I am so very fond of him."

Lady Fairfax regarded Meg solemnly for a moment as if considering carefully what she was about to say. "I think my son drinks too much. I do not like what I have been hearing about him. Nor do I like what you have done, Meg."

"I, Aunt?"

"You know very well I am referring to that young girl you have been introducing about town."

"Gillian?"

"That is her name I believe. You have doubtlessly heard that I exchanged words with her last night and it was most distressing. She had the gall to suggest that I have made my son miserable. Can you imagine the audacity of the creature? And she the natural daughter of Sir Hewitt Gambol! Why, her mother was party to the greatest scandal society has seen in twenty years."

"I am sorry that you do not like Gillian. She is really the most wonderful person. Truly, I have never met anyone so likable. She is kind and considerate and does not put on airs."

"Do not bother to enumerate her virtues. She is a mercenary baggage who is out to ensnare my son into matrimony. I will not have it, Meg. I will not see my family allied to that infamous creature. A girl with such a background could never be Countess of Bain. It is unthinkable." The dowager sighed. "We have many crosses to bear in this life. First, I lost my husband and then my dear Edgar." Her ladyship dabbed her eyes with her handkerchief. "Edgar was everything a son should be, kind and honorable and a worthy successor to his father's title. But Oliver! Oliver has always been a trial to me. He can never take Edgar's place."

"Of course he cannot take his place! My dear Aunt, do not forget that I loved Edgar, too. But he is gone and Oliver remains. Certainly Oliver is not like his brother, just as you and my mother are different. But he is your son, too. He needs you. You must not desert him, for he loves you very much."

"Does he? I doubt that very much."

"You're wrong, Aunt. You are wrong about many things. I pray you will think carefully about this. I implore you to go and see Oliver. Make things right with him."

Lady Bain stared at Meg, who was unsure whether the dowager was going to burst into tears or launch into another tirade. She did neither, but sat quietly and made no reply.

Meg did not know what to do and, fearing to say anything further, took her leave of her unhappy aunt.

Gillian arrived at the Fairfax home and was informed by the butler that Lady Fairfax was out making a call. Gillian thanked the servant for this information and went to her room, where she found Kate Porter straightening her things.

"Where is Mary MacDonald?"

"Oh, Mary is away, miss. Her ladyship has given her permission to visit her cousin for the day."

"Oh, I see. And what is your name?"

"Kate, miss."

"Well, Kate, I would like you to do me a service."

"Yes, miss?"

"Would you be so kind as to go to Mr. Hull and ask him to fetch my emerald necklace? And I should need a small bag of some kind in which I can put the case. Would you be able to find something like that?"

"I think so, miss." Kate left Gillian and smiled. Here was the opportunity she had been waiting for. If she were clever and very careful, she might obtain the tremendous reward Mrs. Stourbridge had promised her.

Stopping by Lady Fairfax's room, Kate peered inside. Her ladyship was known to be exceedingly careless about her jewels. There had been many times when expensive necklaces or earrings were left upon her ladyship's dressing table after she returned from a late night out. The maid looked around and, seeing no one, entered Meg's room. She advanced to the dressing table and was disappointed to find it in perfect order, with nothing of value lying about.

Kate began to search through the room, examining the wardrobe and bureau drawers. Finding nothing, she proceeded into the adjoining sitting room and pulled open the top drawer of Meg's small writing desk. A grin appeared on Kate's face, for there, sitting among the quill pens, was her ladyship's ruby necklace. The maid took the necklace and hid it in the bodice of her dress. She then left the room to find Lady Fairfax's butler.

Gillian sat upon the bed and examined the items Sir Hewitt had given her. In addition to a very fine gold ring, he had found a number of other pieces of jewelry and she had made a list of the prices he had said they should fetch.

If she could obtain such prices, she would have more than enough to pay Mr. Gregson. Then she and Sir Hewitt would go to Devon, where she was certain she could help him clear up some of his other debts. Surely through careful planning and management of the Devon property, the Gambol finances could be put right. Gillian studied her

father's ring and reflected that, despite the elderly
baronet's reluctance to part with it, she was doing the right
thing.

"Miss? I have the necklace." Kate entered the room and
handed the emerald case to Gillian. She opened it and
looked at the necklace.

"Yes, thank you, Kate." Gillian closed the box. "Did
you find me a bag I might carry it in?"

"Yes, miss." Kate produced a cloth bag.

"That should do very nicely." Gillian took the bag and
placed the emerald case inside. She then put Sir Hewitt's
ring and the other pieces in with it. "Now, if you would be
so kind as to help me with my pelisse and bonnet, Kate, I
shall be off."

"Alone, miss?"

"Yes, alone." Kate helped Gillian into the pelisse and
then handed her her bonnet. "Thank you." Gillian turned
to the mirror and tied the ribbons in a bow under her chin.
Kate took advantage of the brief moment in which Gillian
was concentrating on her hat. Under the guise of straightening the bedclothes, she took the cloth bag and slipped
something inside.

"Good day, then, miss," said Kate, handing the cloth
bag to Gillian.

"Thank you, Kate." Gillian glanced once more into the
mirror and then, clutching the cloth bag tightly, left the
room and the house.

eighteen

T he Earl of Bain downed a third glass of claret and then considered filling his glass again. He thought suddenly of Gillian Ashley and frowned. He picked up the wine bottle but then put it down. "Damn," he muttered.

"My lord?" The earl's butler appeared at the doorway of the parlor.

"What is it, Parker?"

"Lady Bain is here and wishes to see you."

"My mother here?"

"I have shown her ladyship to the drawing room, my lord."

"Very good, Parker." The earl tried to hide the surprise he felt. After last night's affair, he had thought his mother would avoid him for weeks, perhaps forever. Bain glanced at his reflection in the mirror and smiled ruefully. Why was he so damned careful about his appearance where his mother was concerned? He straightened his cravat and brushed off his shoulders, reflecting that old habits die hard. Her ladyship had always been quite a stickler for a neat appearance.

The earl entered the drawing room prepared for another unfortunate meeting with the dowager. He hoped he would be able to bear all her reproaches without losing his temper.

"Good day, Oliver."

"Mother." He stood looking at her for a moment and then sat down beside her on the sofa. To his surprise she seemed ill-at-ease.

"I felt I had to talk to you, Oliver. You see, I have just seen your cousin Meg. You know I have always thought her a willful child, and in truth I believe my sister spoiled her terribly. But all that is beside the point.

"I have been thinking about what she said to me, and although most of it was utter nonsense, I have decided that perhaps there is some truth in some of it.

"I know Meg was very fond of Edgar. They were born the same year and were very close, just as you and she are very close. And that Gillian creature. Well, I told Meg what I thought of her sponsoring the girl and Meg acted as if she were the most wonderful person she knew, so I did not get very far.

"Perhaps I should be grateful to the creature for bringing this out into the open, but do not mistake me, I think her rude and ill-bred to have done so. Of course, I suppose I should get to the point."

Bain had been listening to his mother's words with a slightly perplexed expression and was very glad to hear her ladyship's last statement. He waited expectantly.

"The point is that I have been unfair to you. I have thought too much about Edgar, and I suppose I did hold you accountable, knowing full well you had nothing to do with the accident. I should make amends and I am asking you to forgive me."

The earl was thunderstruck.

"Don't stand there gaping at me, Oliver," said the dowager impatiently. "Do you forgive me or not?"

His lordship smiled and embraced his mother.

Mr. William T. Bancroft was very proud of his business establishment. He had taken his father's small jewelry shop and had made it into one of the most profitable businesses in London. He counted all the important members of society among his clientele and was renowned for his sense and discretion.

Mr. Bancroft, therefore, was not too happy at hearing that a young and escorted lady wished to speak to him personally. Reluctantly, he told his clerk to bring her into his private office.

"How do you do, Mr. Bancroft." Gillian Ashley entered the room and extended her hand.

Mr. Bancroft took it and regarded her curiously. He knew a lady of quality when he saw one, and Gillian certainly fitted all his criteria. She was also very lovely, and her bright smile charmed him instantly.

"How might I help you, miss?"

"My name is Miss Ashley." Gillian put the cloth bag on Mr. Bancroft's desk. "I have brought some jewelry that I would like to sell to you."

Mr. Bancroft was about to protest that he did not usually do business this way, but instead he took the bag. He pulled out the case that held the emerald necklace and opened it up. "This is a very beautiful necklace."

"There are some other pieces, Mr. Bancroft. I should like to know what you would give me for them. The necklace is mine and the other pieces belong to my father."

Bancroft was still examining the necklace. "My associate Mr. Smithson is out at the moment and I should like to consult with him. He will be back later this afternoon."

"I do have a number of things I have to do," said Gillian uncertainly. "Do you think you could keep these things and discuss the matter with Mr. Smithson? Then you could contact me concerning the offer you will make. I am staying with Lady Fairfax."

"I am well acquainted with Lady Fairfax. Very well, Miss Ashley, I shall send you word at her ladyship's house as soon as possible."

"I do thank you, Mr. Bancroft, and I shall be expecting to hear from you soon."

"Yes, indeed, miss."

Bancroft escorted Gillian to the door and then returned to his desk, where he took the entire contents of the bag out and studied it piece by piece. Sir Hewitt's ring provoked an appreciative nod, although he dismissed a brooch that had been in the Gambol family for years as ugly and unsalable. "What's this?" A rumpled handkerchief was wrapped around something, and when he pulled it open, a beautiful ruby necklace was revealed.

Mr. Bancroft took the necklace and examined it carefully. "It is the same one," he said aloud. He had recognized it as the same necklace that Lady Meg Fairfax had purchased in his shop some months ago. It was a very expensive and lovely piece, and Bancroft was puzzled. Lady Fairfax was one of his best customers, and he was surprised to see her necklace among those items Miss Ashley was trying to sell. Bancroft gazed down at the ruby necklace in his hand and thought that he had best consult Lady Fairfax herself about the matter.

Meg Fairfax returned home exhausted from her interview with her aunt and two other calls she had made. She entered her house and found herself wishing for a bath and her bed, even though it was not much past one o'clock.

"Where is Miss Ashley, Hull?" asked Meg as she took off her bonnet.

"Miss Ashley returned earlier but went out again, my lady."

"Did she say where she was going?"

"She did not say, my lady."

"I do hope she intends to return for luncheon," said her ladyship.

"She did not say, my lady. There are several letters for your ladyship."

"Indeed? My heavens, there are a good many." Meg took the stack of letters into the drawing room and sat down and started to open them. There was yet another letter from Lord Fairfax saying he would come to town very shortly and a very long letter from Meg's sister in Scotland as well as numerous short notes and invitations. Lady Fairfax perused them all carefully and then looked up to see the butler entering the drawing room.

"Lord Bain is here to see you, my lady."

"Lord Bain? Do show him in, Hull." Meg did not expect her cousin to appear at this hour, but was always glad to see him. She was especially happy to see him looking so cheerful.

"Oliver, you look positively gleeful. You must have some good news."

The earl kissed his cousin on the cheek and sat down beside her. "I must thank you for whatever you said to my mother this morning."

"Good heavens! I thought she quite resented what I said to her. You know she has never liked me."

"She came to me right after you left her. The result is that we are on speaking terms, perhaps even better than that, although I shan't be overly optimistic."

"Oliver, that is good news. But truly I suspect it is Gillian you should thank. I daresay your mother is so formidable that no one ever is courageous enough to speak his mind to her, except Gillian last night."

Bain frowned. "Poor Gillian. I was beastly to her last night."

"You were indeed. I daresay you were quite unreasonable."

"Where is she? I must talk to her."

Meg smiled. "Out, I am sorry to say, but I expect her home soon. You are fond of her, aren't you, Oliver?"

"Now, Meg, don't get any ideas."

"And why not? I do not think the idea of you and

Gillian together is a bad one. I don't know why I didn't think of it before. She is perfect for you and you are a tolerable good fellow. Marry her, Oliver."

"I don't know if she'd have me."

"Then you had best find out. Were I a betting woman, which I am not, I should put my money on her taking you. You are not a bad catch."

He laughed. "I'm not so certain of that, and after last night I doubt if she'll even speak to me."

The butler interrupted them. "There is a gentleman to see you, my lady. A Mr. Bancroft."

"Mr. Bancroft? Not the jeweler? Very well, Hull, show him in." She turned to the earl. "Rather curious of Bancroft to call."

"Perhaps your account is in arrears, Meg."

"It is not," protested Meg, but looked somewhat indignantly at Mr. Bancroft when he walked in the door.

Bancroft bowed to her ladyship and then to the earl. "Thank you for seeing me, my lady. I have a matter of some delicacy to discuss with you."

His lordship turned an amused look at Meg and she frowned. "I am certain that you can say what you have to say to me in front of my cousin Lord Bain."

"Very well, my lady." Bancroft took a small packet from his pocket and opened it up. The contents he handed to Lady Fairfax.

"What in the world?" cried her ladyship. "They are my rubies! Where did you get them?"

Lady Fairfax's reaction seemed to confirm Mr. Bancroft's suspicions. "From a Miss Ashley who came to my shop today. She said she wished to sell the contents of a cloth bag she brought to my establishment. The necklace was in the bag and I recognized it immediately. I thought I should inform your ladyship."

Meg was regarding the necklace curiously and Bain spoke up. "Meg, did you not tell me you thought the clasp on the necklace was faulty? You said you were going to take it back to Mr. Bancroft. Miss Ashley must have taken it for you and forgotten to mention it to Mr. Bancroft.''

"The clasp faulty?" said Mr. Bancroft, somewhat insulted by this reference to his organization's craftsmanship. "Might I see the necklace?" When Meg handed it back to him, he examined the clasp carefully. "I see nothing wrong with it, my lady."

"I am glad to hear it. I suspect it is just the fault of my maid. She is a very clumsy girl. I do thank you for bringing the necklace to me."

"Yes, thank you, Mr. Bancroft," said his lordship. "You are well-known for the quality of your merchandise and"—the earl looked meaningfully at the merchant—"your discretion. You can expect our continued patronage."

Mr. Bancroft caught Bain's meaning immediately and bowed. "I thank your lordship." He glanced over at Meg. "My lady." He bowed to her and then turned and left them.

"Oh, dear, Oliver. What is this all about? Why did Gillian take my rubies? How did she get them? I distinctly remember putting them in my desk drawer. I was going to have Hull lock them up last night, but it was so very late. I didn't even think of them this morning. Mary always takes care of these things, but I gave her the day off. This is all very peculiar, Oliver."

"You cannot think Gillian would have done anything dishonest?"

"Certainly not, but it is rather odd, don't you think? I do wish Gillian would get home so we could untangle this matter."

Her ladyship's words were prophetic for within seconds Gillian returned and, at a word from the butler, came quickly into the drawing room. She saw Bain and met his gaze awkwardly. "Good day, Lord Bain."

"Miss Ashley."

"Gillian, my dear. Do come and sit down. The most curious thing has happened. Mr. Bancroft the jeweler was here."

"Mr. Bancroft was here? Oh, dear, I am sorry that he bothered you. I thought he would send me a note. Did he tell you what price he would give me for the jewels?"

"No, he did not."

"No? That is odd. You see, I brought him my emeralds and some things Sir Hewitt owned. Poor dear, he hated to part with anything. But that terrible Mr. Gregson came again this morning and demanded payment. My father is in quite a bit of trouble, it seems."

"Gillian." Lord Bain looked very serious and Gillian regarded him curiously. "Bancroft brought this necklace to Meg."

Meg held out her rubies and Gillian looked confused. "Why, it is just like the necklace you wore last night."

"Gillian, it *is* the necklace I wore last night. It was in with the things you brought to Mr. Bancroft this morning."

It took a moment for the significance of this statement to reach Gillian. When it did, she stared at Meg incredulously. "You don't think I took your necklace to try to sell it?"

Meg shook her head. "I do not think so for an instant. I did think you may be able to explain how my necklace was with the other things."

"I can't understand it, Meg. But I swear I knew nothing about it."

"Was there anyone else about?" asked Meg.

"Not really. Oh, there was Kate. I asked her to fetch my emeralds from Hull."

"Kate." Meg looked over at Bain. "She is the new parlor maid. Perhaps she would know something." Meg rose and rang for the butler, who appeared immediately.

"Hull, please bring Kate here."

"Kate, my lady?"

"Kate," repeated her ladyship.

A few minutes later the butler appeared with Kate in tow. It was obvious to Bain that Kate was uneasy, and he suspected the answer to the mystery lay with the petite maid.

"Kate," said Gillian, taking the initiative in the interrogation, "do you know anything about a necklace being put into the cloth bag that you fetched for me this morning?"

"Necklace, miss? Why, I did get the emerald necklace for you from Mr. Hull, miss."

"No, Kate," said her ladyship a trifle impatiently. "Not that necklace, another one."

"I don't know what your ladyship could mean."

"I think you do, Kate." Bain looked over at the maid with the stern look that intimidated his own servants.

"No, my lord, I don't know what you mean."

"I think you had best tell us the truth, Kate," continued his lordship. "We know very well that you are behind this. It is a very serious matter."

Kate looked like she was going to burst into tears under Bain's harsh scrutiny, and Gillian felt sorry for the girl.

"Come, Kate, tell us what happened," she said kindly.

Bain's sternness followed by Gillian's sympathetic request caused Kate's resolve to falter. "I am sorry, miss."

"Out with it, girl," demanded Bain. "Did you take Lady Fairfax's necklace?"

"I did, my lord, but someone made me do it."

"And who was that?"

"Mrs. Stourbridge, my lord."

"Mrs. Stourbridge," cried Meg. "Why on earth would she have you do such a thing?"

"Mrs. Stourbridge wanted me to keep an eye on miss and tell her what was happening in the house. I'm sorry, my lady, but I've mouths to feed and Mrs. Stourbridge was paying me right well. I told her and Lady Ashley that miss was talking about selling her jewelry to get money for her father, and Mrs. Stourbridge come up with the idea for me to find a way to make miss look bad to your ladyship.''

"This is monstrous. How could you agree to such a thing?"

"I am sorry, my lady." Tears were streaming down Kate's cheeks and Gillian found it hard to be angry with her. However, the idea that Christobel Stourbridge and her mother would scheme to cause her harm was abhorrent.

Gillian turned to Meg. "Why would they do this? Oh, I know Christobel hates me, but I cannot believe she would stoop to such a thing as this."

"I know they resent your coming out and your great success, and that unfortuante incident at Lady Cavendish's may have caused Christobel to forget her scruples, if indeed she had any to begin with."

"They have no right! Regardless of how they resent me, they have no right to try to destroy your good opinion of me. It is infamous! Well, I shall not allow them to think they have succeeded. I am going to see Lady Ashley and her daughter and force them to answer for this."

Meg Fairfax was growing alarmed by Gillian's expression. "Wait a moment, Gillian. You must not do anything harsh. I do not see what purpose it would serve to confront Lady Ashley and her horrible daughter, especially when you are so angry. I pray you wait and think over the matter. Do calm down, my dear. No harm was done."

"No harm? But, Meg, what must Mr. Bancroft think of me?"

"Bancroft? He is but a jeweler, and very discreet."

Gillian did not seem to be listening. "I am going to see them, Meg."

"Wait, Gillian," said Bain sternly. "Don't be foolish. That temper of yours has got you into trouble before."

Gillian looked up at Bain. "So you are going to reproach me again? Is that why you came here? I shall thank you, sir, to stay out of my affairs."

"Dammit, Gillian, I did not come here to quarrel. You can be the most unreasonable female at times."

"You call me unreasonable? I daresay the word better describes you, my lord. Don't forget how you came in last night accusing me of betraying your confidence without making any attempt to find out what really happened."

"Stop it, both of you," cried Meg. "I will not listen to this silly fighting."

"I am sorry, Meg. Do excuse me. I must go to see Christobel Stourbridge."

"Not this again? Really, Gillian, it is not a good idea. Tell her, Oliver."

"I will tell her nothing," said his lordship angrily.

"Please, Meg, lend me your carriage."

Realizing that her young friend could not be dissuaded, Lady Fairfax threw up her hands. "Oh, very well, but I will go with you. We shall tell Christobel Stourbridge what we think of her reprehensible conduct. Oh, no, I cannot go. I just remembered that Lady Hertford is going to call this afternoon and the prince may accompany her. I cannot very well be absent, and I daresay you should be here, too, Gillian. This matter can wait."

"It cannot wait, Meg. Tell Lady Hertford I regret not seeing her, but I must find Mrs. Stourbridge and Lady Ashley at once. I can go alone. Do not worry, I shall not do anything I would regret."

Meg did not seem convinced of this and appealed once more to Bain. "Oliver, can't you do anything to stop her?"

"I'm afraid not."

Gillian looked over at his lordship. "I am going to see Mrs. Stourbridge. Please excuse me, Meg."

"Then I am going with you." Bain spoke quickly, and

Gillian thought for a moment she had misunderstood.

"You want to come with me, my lord?"

The earl nodded.

"That is a good idea," said Meg. "Someone must restrain you from murdering the women."

"No one need accompany me," said Gillian. "I know, Lord Bain, you have better ways to spend your time."

"I said I wished to go and I will go. My carriage is waiting." Bain spoke so forcefully that Gillian did not argue. She said good-bye to Meg and left the room.

Meg and Bain exchanged a glance then the earl followed after Gillian.

They arrived at the home of Christobel Stourbridge in a few minutes, for it was not very far from the Fairfax residence. Gillian was grateful for the short distance because she found sitting beside his lordship most awkward. They had both sat in silence, regarding each other warily.

When they arrived, Bain noted Gillian looked very angry, and he was unsure whether her anger was directed at Christobel and her mother or at himself. She was very cool to him as he helped her down from the carriage, and he found himself growing increasingly irritated with her.

They were met at the door by a servant who informed them that Mrs. Stourbridge was not at home, nor was Lady Ashley there. Gillian was not at all pleased with this information and demanded to know where the ladies were to be found. The servant, who was rather surprised at the young lady's tone, explained that Mrs. Stourbridge and her mother had gone to Ashley Manor and would not return for a fortnight.

"And where is Ashley Manor?" said Gillian in a commanding voice.

"Why, it is at Woodbridge, miss."

Gillian turned to Bain. "Do you know where this place is, Lord Bain?"

"I do, but you cannot mean to go there. It is some distance, at least fifteen miles from town."

"That is not very far. I would be grateful if you would lend me your carriage."

"Lend you the carriage? I will not. I'll not have you rushing off into the country on a fool's errand."

"Fool's errand, is it? Then I am a fool?"

"Running off to Woodbridge in a temper is foolish."

"Must you always harp about my temper?" Gillian shouted the words and then turned and walked briskly away.

Bain hurried after her. "Gillian, where are you going?"

"To Ashley Manor. I shall hire someone to take me there."

"For God's sake! Oh, very well, I'll take you."

"I could not possibly trouble you, my lord."

"Dammit, Gillian, if you don't get into my carriage, I shall pick you up and toss you in."

Somewhat startled by his vehemence, Gillian hesitated for a moment and then wordlessly returned to Bain's carriage. She did not wait for his assistance, but climbed inside and then sat stiffly on the seat as he climbed in after her.

Bain shouted the destination to his driver, and then, staring grimly at Gillian, he folded his arms across his chest and resolved to say nothing. Gillian stared back at the glowering earl and reflected that it was going to be a very long journey.

nineteen

T hey had traveled nearly seven wordless miles when the rain started. Gillian glanced out the window at the darkened sky and the rain. She then looked at Bain, who was still maintaining his stony silence.

It was a miserable ride, thought Gillian. Her temper had cooled considerably and she was finding the prolonged silence difficult. "Do you think it is much farther, Lord Bain?"

"What?" Bain had been lost in thought.

"Do you think it is much farther to Ashley Manor?"

His lordship shrugged. "I should think we are halfway there at least."

Gillian frowned and made no reply. The ride seemed interminable and she felt increasingly awkward with Bain's silence and the way he kept staring at her.

"Was that the end of the conversation, Miss Ashley?"

"Perhaps it should be. We would only begin to argue."

Bain nodded. "You are probably right." He lapsed into silence again and Gillian watched him with increasing frustration. She then turned her attention to the window and the rain, which was now pouring down.

The road was suddenly worse and Gillian found herself being jolted harshly. Bain shouted for his driver to slow down, but his voice was lost in a clap of thunder. "Damnation," muttered his lordship ill-humoredly as the vehicle bounced and shook violently.

There was a severe jolt as the carriage wheel hit a large rock and it stopped with a lurch. Gillian found herself thrown to the opposite seat and directly into Bain's lap. "Oh, I am sorry," said Gillian, much disconcerted by the press of his lordship's body against her own.

She hastened to pull away from him, but he held her fast. "Are you all right, Gillian?"

"I am fine. Please!" Bain released her and she scrambled back to the other seat just as the door of the carriage was flung open and the very wet driver peered in.

"Beg your pardon, my lord, but that bump was a bad one and I fear there's damage done to one o' the wheels."

"Good God! Can you fix it, Harry?"

"I don't know, my lord, but there be a public house just up the road and I hope to find someone who can help me. I'd best not try to drive it any farther, though, my lord."

Bain looked over at Gillian. "It seems we shall have to walk a bit. Damn the rain."

Gillian looked out the window and saw a rather large and uninviting building a short distance ahead. "I think I can survive such a walk."

"I am gratified to hear it," growled Bain. He alighted from the carriage and waited to help Gillian down.

"Thank you, my lord, but I can manage."

"Very well. I'll not stand here arguing." He walked off, and Gillian climbed down and followed after him.

The rain was coming down in large heavy drops, and by the time they reached the public house, they were both very wet. This did little to improve either of their tempers. They went inside the building and looked around. It was clean and pleasant enough, and a fire burned invitingly in the fireplace. The proprietor, judging by their clothes that they were persons of quality, came eagerly up to them and offered them the hospitality of his establishment.

"Do you have someone who can help my man with the carriage wheel?"

"Aye, sir, my son Jim will see to it. If you and the lady would care to sit down, I could bring you some food and drink."

Gillian found herself hungry at the mention of food and was not averse to the idea of having some refreshment. She sat down at one of the tables. Bain started to sit down, but stopped. "If you don't mind me joining you, madam."

"You may do as you wish."

"Thank you so much." The earl bowed with mocking politeness and sat down. "So you see what you have got us into. Here we are stuck in some filthy provincial inn, God knows where, soaking wet and likely to develop pneumonia."

"So you are blaming me, my lord. By my honor, that is becoming a habit with you and one I do not like very much. And it is not filthy." Gillian removed her wet bonnet and placed it beside her. "You did not have to come, my lord."

Bain started to reply, but the approach of the proprietor stopped him. That worthy man had heard Gillian say "my lord" and was thrilled at having a titled nobleman in his establishment. "What would your lordship wish me to get you and your lady?"

"Anything, damn you! Just hurry up and see that my carriage is seen to."

"Very good, my lord," said the proprietor, retreating hastily.

"Did you have to be so rude?" Gillian demanded. "I am finally seeing the real Bain, am I not? How you love to bully people."

He scowled in reply, and they sat there, wet and miserable. The proprietor rushed to supply them with food and received a black look from Bain for his trouble.

Gillian had by this time lost her appetite and found the

food unappealing. She was glad when Bain's coachman presented a diversion by entering the room soaking wet and approaching them timidly.

"Excuse me, my lord." Bain's coachman stood respectfully, hat in hand. "The wheel's not too bad, my lord, but I've need of another man to help put it right. Two men can't do it. Mr. Phelps, that's the man what's helping me, says there's no one else what can help hereabouts since his father has a bad back. I shall have to go to the village to fetch someone."

"How far is that?"

"A mile or so, my lord."

"Damnation, Harry. I don't want to stay here a moment longer than necessary."

"Then perhaps you might assist Harry, my lord," said Gillian. "That is, if your back will hold out."

Bain frowned ominously. "That is a good idea, Miss Ashley. I would do anything to get this ridiculous mission over more quickly."

"My lord!" The coachman was not at all happy with Gillian's suggestion. "You're a gentleman, my lord, and 'tis no work for a gentleman."

"Then it should suit his lordship well enough," said Gillian.

Bain did not reply, but followed his man out into the rain, leaving Gillian to contemplate the fire and reflect on her feelings for the Earl of Bain. He could be the most stubborn, infuriating man, she thought, and then sighed. She loved him desperately.

A short time later the door opened and two red-coated soldiers entered the room. They shouted for the proprietor to bring them ale, although Gillian suspected they were already close to inebriation. Flagons in hand, they made their way over to the fire. One of them espied Gillian and looked boldly at her.

She looked down at the plate of food, much embarrassed by the soldier's scrutiny. "Well, good day to you, miss," said the soldier, doffing his hat and then tossing it down on the table. "Didn't expect to see a pretty lady like you in here. Not all alone, are you?"

Gillian found herself irritated by the man's familiar manner. "No, I am not alone, sir. I am with a friend."

"I hope it is a lady friend."

"No, I am waiting for a gentleman."

"I'm a gentleman, and so is my friend. Won't we do?"

The other soldier looked embarrassed by his friend's behavior. "Come on, Hatcher, leave the lady in peace."

Hatcher took no notice of his friend's words, but sat down beside Gillian and took a long swallow of ale. "Would your gentleman friend be one of the poor fellows working on the carriage down the road?"

Gillian nodded. "Yes, and he should be here at any moment."

"I don't know about that. It looked like those lads had their work cut out for them."

"I must tell you, sir, that his lordship will not appreciate you taking his seat."

"His lordship, is it?" Hatcher laughed. "Hear that, Camden? His lordship! Who would have thought a lordship would be helping to pull a wheel off a carriage in the pouring rain?"

Gillian's face flushed indignantly. "I will thank you to get up, sir, and take yourself away from me. I do not wish your company."

"Come on, Hatcher," said the other soldier. "Come away from the lady."

"You keep quiet, Camden," he shouted, and then grinned at Gillian. "He's just jealous, but I found you first. Now, what is your name, my dear?"

Gillian said nothing.

"Shy, are you? Well, my name is William Hatcher. You

call me Willy if you like. God, you're a good-looking girl."

"Hatcher, will you stop acting like a jackass!"

"Damn you to hell, Camden! I am your superior officer, if you have forgotten. Go see to the horses."

The other soldier looked helplessly at Gillian and then shrugged and left the room.

"Damned rotter, Camden," muttered Hatcher. "Now where were we? Oh, yes, I was saying what a fine-looking girl you are."

Gillian stood up abruptly. "I will not listen to your ill-mannered comments any longer, Mr. Hatcher. You are no gentleman. That is perfectly clear."

Hatcher slammed his flagon of ale down on the table and stood up. "I am an officer and a gentleman."

"You are a disgrace to your uniform."

It was obvious that William Hatcher was not used to such responses from females. Indeed, he considered himself quite a ladies' man and did not like to see himself rebuffed. "He must be quite a man, this fixer of carriage wheels, miss, but I doubt if he's the equal of Willy Hatcher. And he's not here, while old Willy is. How about giving old Willy a chance to prove himself?"

"You are disgusting."

"That's a bit harsh coming from some carriage fixer's bit of muslin."

Gillian glared at Hatcher and then turned to walk away from him. "Wait a moment, miss," he said, grabbing her arm roughly. "No woman walks away from old Willy."

"Let go of me!" shouted Gillian, but Hatcher pulled her to him and tried to kiss her. Gillian struggled to extricate herself from his grasp and shouted, "Help, help, Bain!"

The earl, who had finished with the carriage wheel and was soaking wet and even more ill-tempered, entered the public house just as Gillian shouted.

"God in heaven!" he cried, and rushed to Gillian's aid.

William Hatcher felt two strong hands grab his shoulders, and he was jerked backward and spun around. He had barely enough time to gape in horror when Bain's fist connected with his jaw and he fell heavily to the ground.

Hauling the soldier to his feet, Bain sent him flying across the room. He landed in a seeming lifeless heap on the floor, but the earl did not seem at all concerned about his condition. "Gillian, are you all right?"

The concern on his face made Gillian forget all their quarrels. She rushed over to him and was engulfed in his embrace. "Oh, Bain," she said, pressing her face against his chest. "I was so frightened."

"Did he hurt you? If he did, I shall kill him, if I haven't done so already."

Gillian looked questioningly into his eyes. He leaned down and, pulling her close, crushed his mouth against hers. Gillian was at first too startled to respond, but then returned his kiss with long-suppressed ardor.

She felt a strange new thrill pass through her body as Bain's lips devoured hers and then moved hungrily down along her neck to the fullness of her breasts. She gasped with pleasure as he lingered there, one hand caressing her breast through the flimsy fabric of her gown.

"What the devil!" A masculine voice brought Bain and Gillian to their senses, and they looked over to see the soldier Camden staring horror-struck at the prone form of his companion. "What is going on here?"

"Do you know this man?" demanded Bain, still holding Gillian firmly in his arms.

"He's my captain, sir."

"Then I suggest you attend to him, Lieutenant."

"You are accountable for his injuries, sir. He is an officer in the king's army."

"And a damned bounder. I shall see him tossed out of

the king's service." Bain and Gillian reluctantly separated.

William Hatcher moaned and his fellow soldier knelt down beside him. "Are you all right, old man?"

Hatcher rubbed his jaw. "God, Camden, it hurts like hell."

"But you can move it. Thank God it's not broken." Camden looked over at Bain. "You shall have to answer for this, sir."

"I shall have to answer to nothing."

Camden was taken aback by Bain's arrogant tone. "Might I have the privilege of knowing whom I am addressing?"

"You may indeed. I am the Earl of Bain."

Lieutenant Camden was sufficiently versed in knowledge of his country's peers to know that the Earl of Bain was a very wealthy and powerful man. "I am sorry, my lord. I didn't know—"

"That is enough, Lieutenant. Get your captain out of my sight or I shall see to it his commanding officer knows exactly what has happened."

Camden thought retreat well advised and helped his comrade to his feet. He then assisted the still-shaky Hatcher out of the room.

Bain smiled at Gillian. "Amazing what the mention of a man's commanding officer can do."

"I think the mention of your name was quite sufficient."

"I should have the fellow tossed out of the army."

"I think, my lord, that he has learned his lesson. Oh, Bain, I have been such an idiot."

"My darling Gillian, it is I who has been the idiot. Forgive me for everything."

"Oh, Bain, I love you. I was certain you hated me."

He took her hand. "Hated you? Gillian, I think I loved you since that first time I saw you."

"You did?"

He smiled. "It's true, although I didn't realize it at first. I know damn little about love, it seems. How could I help but love you? You are the most adorable and the most maddening woman in the world."

"Oh, Bain!" Gillian threw her arms around the earl's neck. "I still cannot believe it."

"Is it so odd as that? Didn't you have even a hint of how I felt?"

Gillian looked earnestly up at his lordship. "It is just that I feared you were in love with someone else."

"My darling, I have never loved anyone until I met you."

"Oh, Bain, I am so glad."

"But you, my dear Gillian, what of all those young suitors of yours?"

"I love you, and only you. How could I be interested in anyone else when I have you to compare them with?"

"What utter nonsense!" Bain laughed but grew suddenly serious. "Did you really think I loved someone else?"

Gillian looked down. "I was led to believe . . . No, I should not even mention it."

"No, tell me. I think we had best be honest with each other."

Gillian paused before she replied. "There was a certain lady who told me that you were . . . you were in love with her. Bain, I know that gentlemen sometimes have . . . mistresses, and I could not bear the thought that you and she—"

"Good God, Gillian, who was it?"

"Mrs. Colville."

Bain stared at her, quite astonished. "Henrietta Colville told you that she and I . . . ?"

Gillian nodded. "She made it very clear, and she is so beautiful."

"Gillian, my darling, look at me. I have not been a

saint, Gods knows, but upon my honor as a gentleman, I have never taken Henrietta Colville to bed. And I have never ever loved anyone but you. You must believe that."

Gillian looked searchingly into his eyes. "I do believe you."

"Then say you'll marry me."

"Oh, Bain, I want nothing else in the world but to be your wife." Gillian smiled and started to embrace his lordship, but had a sudden thought. "But, dearest Bain, what will your mother say? She detests me."

Bain grinned and pulled her to him. "Gillian, my love, I can honestly say that I do not give a damn what she thinks." His lordship did not give Gillian opportunity for reply, but covered her mouth with kisses.

twenty

T he rain had stopped as suddenly as it had come and the sun peered tentatively out from behind the clouds. Gillian Ashley found herself once again in the earl's carriage, but this time she paid little attention to the passing scenery. She remained locked in Bain's embrace as he murmured endearments and pronounced himself to be the happiest man in the kingdom.

"Must you still see Lady Ashley, Gillian? I am eager to get back to London to see if Sir Hewitt will approve of me."

"Approve? I daresay he will be thrilled. Indeed, I thought he was going to force you to marry me at gunpoint. Poor Bain. Are you certain you want to ally yourself with me and my scandalous family?"

"Very certain, my love," he said, planting a kiss on her nose.

She laughed and kissed his cheek. "I do want to get back to town, but I do want to see Lady Ashley. I must clear up this matter."

"Very well, my lady. We shall see the Ashleys." He glanced out the carriage window. "Very pretty country, but I like the scenery inside far better."

She smiled and embraced him again.

* * *

Having taken care to get very exact directions to Ashley Manor from the proprietor at the inn, Harry expertly turned the horses into the narrow lane leading to the stately country home. Soon Bain's coach came to a halt in front of Ashley Manor.

Inside the carriage, Gillian was extricating herself from his lordship's embrace and patting her hair. "We have arrived, it seems," he said matter-of-factly.

Bain, who was no more enthused about the venture than when they left London, got out of the carriage and helped Gillian down.

"So this is Ashley Manor," said Gillian, studying the massive stone front of the impressive Tudor structure. This was where her mother had lived for those unhappy years of her marriage to Lord Ashley. She had never been able to talk of her life here, but Gillian knew it had been miserable.

It was a very beautiful house with well-manicured grounds that attested to the skill and efficiency of the groundskeepers. The topiary trees were clipped to perfection and the grass was brilliantly green and welltrimmed.

Gillian took Bain's arm and the two of them walked up to the front door, where Bain lifted an enormous antique door knocker and allowed it to fall with a thud. The door was opened by a gray-haired servant who looked first at Bain and then at Gillian. When he saw Gillian, his mouth flew open in bewilderment. "My lady? No, it cannot be." He continued to stare at Gillian as if she were a ghost.

"Would you cease your gaping, man," said his lordship irritably. "Inform Lady Ashley that Miss Gillian Ashley and Lord Bain are here to see her. Here is my card."

The servant continued to stare at Gillian but took Bain's card with a shaky hand. "Very well, my lord," he said, hurrying away without ushering them inside or closing the door.

The earl and Gillian exchanged glances and then stepped inside the entryway. There was a lovely oak stairway and many antique pieces of furniture as well as tapestries, paintings, and the obligatory suit of armor in the corner.

"Such a peculiar man," said Gillian, perplexed by their reception. "He looked at me so strangely."

"I shouldn't worry about that. These country fellows can be dashed odd. I daresay the old man was simply overcome by your beauty."

Gillian laughed. "Such rot, Bain. More likely he had an attack of indigestion." She looked across the entry hall. "It is a fine house and that is a lovely painting." Gillian gestured toward a landscape that was hanging near the stairway, and she and Bain walked over to it.

Bain regarded it solemnly. "Yes, that is very good," he pronounced.

"And look at these portraits." Gillian pointed toward a row of paintings hanging along the stairway. "The Ashley ancestors. They seem a very grim lot, don't they?" Gillian looked from one painting to another until her eye fell upon one more recent work and she gasped. "Oh, Bain!"

"What is it, Gillian?" said his lordship, alarmed by her expression.

"That painting. There on the landing."

Bain followed her gaze, and when he espied the painting, he knew immediately what had provoked Gillian's response. He also knew why the old servant had stared so at Gillian. It was a portrait of a young girl, and her face resembled that of Gillian Ashley so closely that he would have sworn it was indeed a picture of Gillian.

"How can it be? Oh, Bain, do you see it?" She hurried up the stairway and, once close to the painting, read the small brass plate affixed to it. "Kathryn Ashley, 1776-1792, daughter of Kenneth, 3rd Viscount Ashley, and beloved sister of Rowland, 4th Viscount."

Bain followed Gillian up the stairs, and his glance went

from the portrait to Gillian's face and then back to the portrait. The resemblance was uncanny and the truth was obvious. Gillian was the daughter of Rowland Ashley. It was suddenly clear to his lordship why Lady Ashley and Christobel Stourbridge had taken such a dislike to Gillian. They were well aware that she resembled the portrait and knew all along her parentage.

"It is like looking in a mirror," said Gillian, reaching out for Bain's hand. "Oh, Bain, could this mean what I think?"

His lordship nodded. "The resemblance is too close for coincidence. It appears, my darling, that you are truly an Ashley."

"It can't be true," said Gillian. "It can't be true."

Bain pressed her hand. "I fear it is true, Gillian."

"What are you doing?" An angry feminine voice came from the foot of the stairs. "Dear God!" As Gillian turned to look at her, Lady Ashley got a good view of her unwelcome visitor standing beside the portrait. The likeness was even more apparent than she had feared.

"Lady Ashley," said Gillian coldly. "Or perhaps I should call you stepmother."

"You are talking nonsense."

"You knew before, didn't you?" Gillian stared down at Lady Ashley. Christobel Stourbridge had joined her mother, and both ladies were regarding Gillian with undisguised malice.

"I don't know what you are talking about," said Lady Ashley.

"I suggest you both leave," said Christobel. "You are unwelcome here."

Gillian descended the stairs and faced her two adversaries. "I understand it all now. The portrait makes it very clear. She was my aunt and Lord Ashley is my father."

"Hewitt Gambol is your father," snarled Christobel,

"and some slight resemblance to a poorly done portrait does not change it."

"In God's name, woman," said Bain. "Some slight resemblance? Any fool would see it, and your treatment of Gillian provides further evidence."

"I don't know what you mean, sir."

"You know very well, madam. Your plan to make us believe Gillian a thief was most inept."

"I didn't know why you would do such a thing," said Gillian. "That is why I came here, to demand an explanation from you. Now I have seen the portrait, it seems no explanation is necessary. It is very clear. You knew all along that I was an Ashley and you were afraid that Lord Ashley . . . that my father would find out the truth. Did you fear for your inheritance, Mrs. Stourbridge?" Gillian shook her head. "You disgust me, both of you. I care nothing for the Ashley name or the Ashley fortune. I have already gained a father and do not need another one."

"In that case, I hope you will go before my husband sees you. He is not a well man. The shock would not be good for him."

"Do not waste your breath, Mama," said Christobel angrily. "Despite what she says, she will not hesitate to try to claim her share of Papa's fortune."

"You are wrong, Christobel," said Gillian with a calmness that surprised his lordship. "I want nothing from any of you, and I do not wish to have any connection with this family. I know how cruelly Lord Ashley treated my mother and I want nothing to do with him or any of you. But I warn you both. If you dare to slander me again, I shall make the truth known to everyone." She looked over at Bain. "Please, Bain, I wish to go away from here."

Bain looked grimly at Lady Ashley and her daughter, but said nothing. He put his arm around Gillian and started to lead her to the door. They had got halfway across the entry hall when a voice called out. "Wait!"

Gillian and Bain stopped and turned around. There standing before them was a white-haired gentleman with very erect posture, who took a pair of spectacles from his pocket and placed them on his nose. Looking at Gillian, he started visibly.

"I am Lord Ashley and I demand to know who you are."

Gillian regarded Lord Ashley intently and then replied. "I was just leaving, sir. Good day to you."

"But who are you? What is your name?"

Gillian looked over at Bain and then at the viscount. "My name is Gillian, Gillian . . . Gambol. Good day to you."

She turned and walked to the door. Bain followed quickly after her. "Gillian, wait."

"No, please, Bain. I don't wish to talk to him. Please, I want to go back to London."

Bain nodded and escorted Gillian outside. He helped her into the carriage and shouted to his driver. "Back to town, Harry. And hurry up!"

"Aye, my lord!" The driver whipped the horses and the carriage started off.

Bain turned to Gillian, his face filled with concern. "Are you all right, Gillian?"

Gillian looked up into his lordship's face and nodded. Wordlessly, Bain took her into his arms and she burst into tears, sobbing against his shoulder.

twenty-one

"Gillian! Bain! Where have you been?" Meg Fairfax embraced Gillian and then frowned at them both. "I have been so worried! What was I to think when you didn't return yesterday? You might well imagine how I felt. And here you are, looking, if I may say so, a trifle disheveled."

"Oh, Meg, I am sorry. I must look a sight. Do allow me to go change."

"I will not, Gillian, not until you tell me what has happened. Come into the drawing room and sit down. I want to know everything."

Gillian and Bain exchanged what Meg thought was a conspiratorial glance but followed her obediently into the drawing room, where they sat down on the sofa.

Lady Fairfax sat down across from them. "Very well, I await your explanation. And I might warn you that I expect it to be a good one. It will not do, Bain, for you to go off somewhere with a respectable young lady and return some thirty hours later."

Bain smiled at Gillian. "Indeed, the young lady's reputation is in jeopardy. It seems I have no recourse but to marry her."

"What!" Meg Fairfax looked quite startled, and Gillian and Bain burst into laughter.

"Oh, Meg, don't look at us like that," said Gillian. She took his lordship's hand. "Bain has asked me to marry him and I accepted before he could change his mind."

"The devil!" cried Meg, totally unconcerned at uttering this unladylike expression. She grinned. "Oh, I am happy for you both. I know you are very well-suited." She rose from her chair and embraced Gillian and then Bain. "This is so marvelous. I do wish you happiness."

"Thank you, cousin," said Bain. "I have ensnared a remarkable young lady."

Meg Fairfax patted their hands fondly and then sat back down on her chair. "This is all quite wonderful, but I must not forget that I am owed an explanation. What happened yesterday?"

"You see, Meg," began Gillian. "Lady Ashley and Christobel were not at home when we arrived. They had gone to their home in the country. You remember that I was in a terrible temper—"

"I do, indeed," commented Meg.

"And I insisted on going to Ashley Manor to find them. Poor Bain came with me and I was perfectly odious to him." She looked over at the earl and grinned. "There was a mishap with the carriage and we took shelter in a public house. It was wet and we were both in terrible tempers and . . ." She looked over at Bain. "And it was the most wonderful day of my life."

"Do go on," said Meg impatiently. "I'm not at all sure if you are making any sense, Gillian. Did you get to Ashley Manor?"

"Yes, we did, Meg. And when we were waiting in the entry hall, I espied the portrait!"

"Portrait? What portrait?"

Lord Bain took Gillian's hand. "You see, Meg, there was a portrait of a young lady, Lord Ashley's sister, who died some years ago. Her resemblance to Gillian was uncanny."

"Good heavens!"

"It appears, Meg," said Gillian, "that I am Rowland Ashley's daughter, after all. That is why Lady Ashley hated me so. She knew all along that I resembled the Ashleys far too much for coincidence. She and Christobel feared that I would find out somehow and claim my inheritance."

"Did you see Lord Ashley?"

"Only for a moment. I did not wish to see him at all. I can never forgive him for the way he treated my mother, and I never want to see him or that wretched Ashley Manor again."

"Oh, Gillian, this must have been a severe trial for you."

Gillian shrugged. "I was so confused at first, Meg, but now I realize that it is something I must accept. What worries me most is that I do not know how I can tell Papa. He will be heartbroken."

"Oh, dear. Sir Hewitt. What will you do?"

"We have discussed it, Bain and I, and I have no choice but to tell him. I cannot deceive him. I shall go see him tonight, for if I put it off any longer, I don't know how I will be able to do it."

Meg nodded. "I know that is best, my dear. Poor Sir Hewitt. He loves you very much. But you look exhausted, Gillian. You must go up and rest now."

Gillian nodded. "I am tired." She looked at Bain. "You will come with me to see Papa?"

"Of course, my darling. I shall go and see to things at my house and be back this evening." He raised her hand to his lips and kissed it, and then Gillian left them to go to her room.

Meg regarded Bain shewdly. "You're getting a fine girl, Oliver. I think even my aunt will realize that in time."

Bain smiled. "Perhaps, but we shall do very well in any case. I love her, Meg, more than I have ever thought it possible to love."

"I'm so glad for you, Oliver." Meg Fairfax leaned over and kissed her cousin on the cheek. "I know you will be happy."

"Thank you, my dear Meg. And now I must be going."

Meg Fairfax watched her favorite cousin leave the room and reflected that things did indeed have a way of working out. She hoped this would be the case when Gillian explained the truth to Sir Hewitt Gambol.

Sir Hewitt looked up eagerly at the sound of someone knocking at his door and shouted impatiently for his man Moffat to open it. His joy at seeing Gillian was unmistakable. "Gillian, my girl!"

"Papa." Gillian hurried over to him and threw her arms around his neck. "Oh, Papa."

Sir Hewitt was puzzled by Gillian's emotional greeting and, after extricating himself from her embrace, regarded her curiously. "Is something wrong, my dear?" He noticed Bain for the first time. "Oh, you're here, too, Bain?"

"Yes, good evening to you, Sir Hewitt."

"Well, sit down, both of you. What is it, Gillian? Is something wrong?"

Bain, who had just sat down in a chair, rose abruptly. "Gillian, I think it would be best if I left you alone."

"Thank you, Bain."

The earl smiled encouragingly and left the room.

The baronet looked somewhat alarmed. "What is it, Gillian? Something is wrong. Is it that fellow Bain? If he has hurt you, I shall run him through with my sword."

"Oh, no, Papa. Bain is wonderful. Indeed, he has asked me to marry him."

"Damn me if I didn't know he'd come to his senses. I'll want a few words with him. He'd better be able to take care of my daughter well enough."

Gillian took Sir Hewitt's hand. "I have to tell you something. It is important. But first I must tell you that you are the only father I have ever had, and I love you dearly. You must believe that."

Sir Hewitt looked apprehensively at Gillian. "What is it, Gillian? What is the matter?"

"You see, Papa, it has to do with the Ashleys. It seems Lady Ashley has hated me."

"The witch!" cried Sir Hewitt.

"Oh, I knew why she should dislike me, but I never could understand the vehemence of her dislike. Indeed, she even attempted to turn Meg Fairfax against me by trying to make Meg believe I had stolen a valuable necklace of hers."

"The damned harpy! How dare she!"

"When I learned of this, I went to see her. She was at the Ashley country home." Gillian paused. "I discovered something when I was there, the reason she has hated me so much."

"What is it?"

"Oh, Papa. It seems that there is evidence pointing to the fact that I am Rowland Ashley's daughter after all."

"What!" Sir Hewitt looked astonished. "That's not possible! You are a Gambol as certain as the sun rises."

"Papa, there was a portrait there at Ashley Manor of Rowland Ashley's sister, who died when she was but sixteen. There was no mistaking the resemblance between me and the girl in the portrait."

"Is that all, a resemblance to a portrait? Why, my girl, you are as like my grandmother as anyone could be."

"No, Papa, I fear that it is true. I am Lord Ashley's daughter."

Sir Hewitt Gambol looked at her for a moment and then turned away. "How can you tell me this? You don't wish to be my daughter?"

"Oh, Papa, of course I do. Can you think that I am glad

to be the daughter of Rowland Ashley? I have come to love you dearly. But I had to tell you. I could not deceive you. I could not go on taking things from you. I have no right."

Tears were steaming down the old gentleman's face. "You are everything to me, Gillian. I cannot bear to lose you now."

"You don't have to lose me. I would still be your daughter, if you would have me." By this time Gillian was herself in tears, and when Bain reentered Sir Hewitt's parlor, he found Gillian and the baronet dabbing their eyes with handkerchiefs and looking fondly at each other.

"I am so sorry, Sir Hewitt," ventured the earl. "I know how you must feel, but you must know that Gillian loves you as much as anyone could love a father."

Sir Hewitt tried valiantly to mask his emotions. "There is no proof anyway. Don't a man's feelings count for anything? I'll not give up my only daughter so easily."

"He has not tossed me out, Bain. He will still have me, it seems."

"Indeed I will, and you'll have me for a father-in-law, my boy. I think it might be a good time to discuss the marriage settlement."

"Oh, Papa!" Gillian found herself blushing and was glad when a knock on the door provided a diversion. Sir Hewitt's servant Moffat hastened to the door and returned with a white-haired gentleman.

"So you are here!" the white-haired gentleman cried, looking at Gillian and Bain.

"Good God!" said Bain, and Gillian regarded the newcomer with stricken expression. There standing before them was Rowland Ashley.

"I want to settle this matter. My wife told me everything, how you humiliated her and plotted to steal my daughter's inheritance."

"What in the name of all the demons of hell," shouted Sir Hewitt. "By the great hound! You are Rowland

Ashley! You damned bounder! Get out of my house at once!"

"I'll get out when I have had my say, Gambol. I have come all this way to settle the matter. This young woman, this Miss Gambol, has no claim to my fortune or my estates."

"God in heaven, man," said Bain, his face reddening in anger, "she is obviously your eldest daughter. Look at her! You cannot help but know it."

"She is not my daughter, sir. No daughter of Caroline Guildford is a daughter of mine. That woman ruined my life, and I shall not allow her daughter to ruin my family's happiness. You may resemble my dear sister in looks, madam, but I know that you are like your mother in deceit and treachery."

At these words Sir Hewitt leapt to his feet and, seemingly oblivious to his gout-stricken foot, ran across the room and pulled his antique saber from the wall. Brandishing this fearsome weapon above his head, he ran toward Lord Ashley. "You're no gentleman, Ashley. You're a liar and a scoundrel. I wish I'd killed you when I had the chance. Take up a sword and we shall settle this once and for all! If you've no stomach for it, you may choose pistols, although they did you no good when last we met."

Lord Ashley, convinced that he was confronted by a madman, turned white with terror. "You are insane, Gambol!"

"Oh, Papa, please stop!"

Bain stepped in and deftly took the sword from Sir Hewitt. "I beg you, sir, calm yourself."

"Please, Papa! Sit down, please."

Sir Hewitt glared at Bain. "Traitor," he muttered. "Ashley, I shall meet you on the field of honor."

"Indeed, Sir Hewitt, I doubt Lord Ashley belongs on the field of honor." Bain put a restraining arm around Sir Hewitt, who had been somewhat appeased by the earl's comment. "Ashley, I urge you to leave us while you still can."

"And who are you, sir?"

"I am the Earl of Bain, and I am soon to wed this lady. Therefore, I will not abide any insults to her. You have my word that she is not interested in your fortune. If you inquire, you will learn that I certainly have no need of it. We will have nothing further to do with you. Get out of this house, sir, or I shall give Sir Hewitt his sword. You are acquainted with his prowess with weaponry, I believe."

Rowland Ashley glared at Bain and then at Gillian and Sir Hewitt. "You're mad, the whole lot of you! And all of you can go to the devil!"

"Get out, you ill-bred coward, you traitorous rogue. God forgive me for not putting that pistol ball through your villainous heart."

"Papa!" cried Gillian, trying to restrain Sir Hewitt.

Rowland Ashley seemed finally convinced it was wisest to depart and he retreated hastily.

"Papa, are you all right?"

"Yes, my dear girl. I should have killed him. Twenty years ago, I missed my opportunity. I wish I had done it today."

"I fear, Sir Hewitt," said Bain, "that it would have been a bit awkward for you had you done so."

Sir Hewitt nodded. "I suspect you are right, my boy. But evidence or no, that man could not have fathered my Gillian. Damn me, I often think it odd that I could have done so, but Ashley? Why, that is impossible! The man is a viper."

Sir Hewitt looked over at Bain. "You should consider yourself lucky, my boy, that you'll not have him for a father-in-law."

Bain and Gillian exchanged glances and burst into laughter.

epilogue

There was a festive mood among the servants at Castle Bain, for her ladyship, the new countess, had given birth to a son. It was well known that his lordship, for all his apparent calm, was ecstatic over the arrival of his heir and the good health of her ladyship.

The morning after the birth of her son, Gillian lay in the canopied ancestral bed and looked down at the infant who was snuggling against her breast.

"Gillian?" Bain entered the room.

"Oh, darling." Gillian extended one hand to him and the earl hurried to her side and sat down on the bed. "Isn't he adorable?"

"It is you who is adorable, my lady," said Bain, kissing her gently on the lips. "How do you feel?"

"A little tired, but very well. As is our son. He looks like you, don't you think?"

Bain laughed. "I certainly hope not."

Gillian smiled mischievously. "It is just that I want no doubts as to his parentage. I have had enough of that sort of thing."

"My dear Gillian, I fear there can be no doubt of his parentage." The earl kissed her again. "You know, Gillian, I never before believed in miracles, but now it seems I have personally witnessed three of them."

"Three, my lord?"

"The first is that I found someone as wonderful as you."

"Such nonsense!"

"And the second one is that little creature there, our son."

"Now I will agree to that. And the third?"

Bain smiled. "The third is that my mother is so happy here at Castle Bain. She is a changed woman."

"And do not forget my papa. He is still another miracle. I can scarcely believe that little over a year ago he could hardly walk. He looks years younger."

"It is because of the love you have given him."

"And also because of your generosity, my sweet Bain, in settling his debts. You are the most wonderful man in the entire world."

"Rubbish," muttered Bain, leaning over to kiss his countess again.

"Oh, excuse me." A feminine voice came from the doorway. "I do not mean to intrude, but I would like to see my grandson."

"Do come in, Mother," said Bain.

The dowager countess entered the room. Having finally abandoned her black mourning clothes, the dowager was dressed in a very becoming green dress. "My dear Gillian," she said, "you look lovely, and just look at this little fellow." The dowager cast a fond grandmotherly gaze at the boy. "He is so handsome and closely resembles you, Oliver."

Bain grinned. "That is my wife's opinion."

"And Gillian is right, as she is so often."

Gillian smiled up at her mother-in-law and thanked Providence that she and the dowager were getting on so well. In truth, the dowager had grown very fond of Gillian, despite her initial disapproval of the match.

"Gillian, my girl!" The booming voice of Sir Hewitt

Gambol was quickly followed by the appearance of that elderly gentleman. Anyone who had not seen the baronet for a year would not have recognized him, for his transformation was quite astonishing. His nose remained a trifle red, but he had lost much weight and looked healthy and almost handsome.

The dowager countess cast a disapproving look at Sir Hewitt as he hurried in, for her acceptance of Gillian did not extend to Sir Hewitt. Yet the dowager Lady Bain managed to adopt an attitude of cool civility toward the baronet, knowing that there was no way to get rid of the man and that she must somehow tolerate him.

Sir Hewitt took no notice of the dowager countess, but devoted his attention to the tiny baby beside Gillian. "I knew it," cried Sir Hewitt happily. "The Gambol blood will out! He's the image of my grandfather. Yes, indeed, he's got the Gambol eyes. Oh, he'll be a handsome rogue one day."

"Sir Hewitt," said the dowager severely, "that baby is very much a Bain. He looks exactly like my son Oliver did when he was a baby."

Before the baronet could reply, Gillian hastened to avert a quarrel. "Oh, please, I do not know who this young gentleman resembles, but he is a very, very beautiful baby."

"That he is," said Bain, "and I think we had best change the subject."

The dowager nodded gravely, and she and Sir Hewitt stood for a few minutes longer admiring the baby and chatting quite civilly.

When they had gone, Bain took his wife's hand. "Do you think they will ever get along, Gillian?"

"I am afraid not, my darling, but at least your mother seems to be growing more tolerant."

Bain smiled. "You may be a trifle optimistic, my lady,

but it is true that I no longer fear my mother is going to poison Sir Hewitt's tea.''

"Bain!''

They both burst into laughter. Then Bain leaned over and gazed adoringly into Gillian's blue eyes. "I love you so much, my dear Gillian.''

"Oh, Bain,'' murmured Gillian, extending her arms to receive his embrace.

about the author

M argaret Summerville grew up in the Chicago area and holds degrees in journalism and library science. Employed as a librarian, she is single and lives in Morris, Illinois, with her Welsh corgi, Morgan. SCANDAL'S DAUGHTER is Ms. Summerville's first Signet Regency.